The Disappearance of Mr. James Phillimore

A Sebastian McCabe – Jeff Cody Mystery

Dan Andriacco

Paperback ISBN 9781780924564
ePub ISBN 9781780924571
PDF ISBN 9781780924588

Published in the UK by MX Publishing
335 Princess Park Manor, Royal Drive,
London, N11 3GX
www.mxpublishing.com
Cover design by www.staunch.com

This book is dedicated to

STEVE AND BARBARA WINTER

in memory of our adventures in England
(but we'll always have Paris)

CONTENTS

Short Story Bonus!
The Adventure of the Vatican Cameos

Chapter One
Deadly Hall

Welles Faro, the *Daily Eye* tabloid columnist, and Sebastian McCabe had been friendly rivals for years. But they'd never actually met until Mac went to London for the debate. If Lynda and I hadn't been in London, too, on the second leg of our honeymoon, we never would have gotten caught up in the murders.

But I'm getting ahead of myself, as usual. The disappearance came first.

On the morning of our second day in London, I regarded my full English breakfast of back bacon, eggs, grilled tomatoes, pan-fried mushrooms, baked beans, toast with butter, sausage, and tea with a critical eye.

"What—no kippers?" I asked my bride of twelve days.

"You wouldn't eat them anyway," Lynda said, accurately. "But what you're really thinking is that almost everything on your plate is fried and you're afraid that if you eat it all you'll be dead of a heart attack in, like, twelve seconds." She knows Jeff Cody so well. "You could have had yogurt and porridge, you know."

"Are you kidding? If I have to pay sixteen pounds for breakfast, I'm going to make it worthwhile even if it kills me. And it might." *No, I am not cheap; I'm thrifty.* I shoveled in some eggs. "This isn't so bad," I added. "I was getting a little tired of Italian pastries for breakfast. And that's not exactly health food, either."

Not that I was complaining about the all-too-short sojourn in Rome, Florence, and Venice during our first week as a married couple. It was glorious. Curly, honey-blond hair and English surname (Teal) notwithstanding, Lynda is half-Italian and fully fluent in that most melodious of languages. Being with her in the country where she had spent her summers growing up was like traveling with my own personal tour guide.

Plus, we were newlyweds. And we were alone then. As I said, glorious.

Now we were camped out at the elegant King Charles Hotel in the heart of London with my best friend, Sebastian McCabe, and his wife, who happens to be my sister, Kate. Mac, who has no concept of money as a limited commodity, had chosen the digs. A main reason seemed to be the many references to the nearby Charing Cross area in what he reverently refers to as the Canon—i.e., the Sherlock Holmes stories. "Why, the agent Hugo Oberstein was captured right in the smoking room of the Charing Cross Hotel in 'The Adventure of the Bruce-Partington Plans'!" he'd informed me, eyes aglow. I suppose we would have stayed there if there'd been an opening.

I looked around the bright, classy surroundings of the restaurant and told myself it was a good thing that my freshly minted wife was so well compensated for her executive position with the nefarious Main Stream Media, Ohio division.

Lynda reached over and took my left hand, the one that didn't have a fork in it. "Thank you for such a wonderful honeymoon, *tesoro mio*," she said in her husky voice. "I know we'll always treasure every magic moment."

So, hang the cost! In a New York minute I was lost in my beloved's deep brown eyes flecked with gold. Lynda's nose is a little crooked and she isn't as beautiful as her world-famous mother, but that's the face I want to wake up with every day for the rest of my life. Her smile and her curve-hugging bright yellow dress with the scoop neckline was all the sun I needed on this rainy London day. Just as I was about to say so, or some similar expression of romantic tenderness, I heard a booming voice coming from behind us and moving our way.

"Ah, the honeymooners—fueling up early, I see!"

"Don't worry," I assured him. "We left you some. Shame about the kippers, though."

Mac raised an eyebrow inquiringly. I kept eating.

Sebastian McCabe is three inches shorter than my six-one, but big in the other direction. If he isn't quite a hundred pounds overweight as I've estimated elsewhere, he's close to it. You may have recognized his bearded face from the photo on the dust jackets of his many best-selling mystery novels or from his occasional appearances on television hawking those fairy tales. Even on vacation he was wearing his trademark bow tie and a sport coat.

He and Kate sat down at our table.

"How'd you two sleep last night?" my sister asked Lynda and me. *Do you really want to ask a couple of honeymooners that, sis?*

Almost as tall as I am, and with the same shade of red hair but a lot more of it, Kate is my protective big sister. In fact, it was a relief to have Lynda around to protect me from her protectiveness.

Once we had discussed the firmness of the mattresses, the size of the beds (and rooms), the pressure of the water coming out of the showerhead, and all the other earth-shattering issues that traveling couples talk about the morning after their first night in a new place, I asked how the three McCabe children were faring under the watchful eye of Mac's parents back in Ohio.

"They're never more than a text away," Kate said.

"Mrs. McCabe texts a lot?" Lynda asked.

Kate shook her head. "No, the kids do, especially—"

She was probably going to say Brian, age eight, but Mac's smartphone cut her off. It's hard to keep talking over a ringtone of *Ride of the Valkyries*.

"Yes," Mac answered. "Oh, good morning, Welles." He listened for a while, and then said: "We'd be delighted! Thank you for arranging it. What time? See you then, my good fellow!"

The gist of that was pretty clear, but Mac spelled it out after he'd hung up. "Faro has arranged for us to have an informal lunch with Arthur James Phillimore at a pub near his home. He will drive us there. I must confess I am most eager to examine that notebook that Phillimore has acquired."

You'd probably heard of Phillimore, investment guru to the stars, even before the hubbub that summer. I certainly had, and I was looking forward to meeting him. He was the financial whiz that Hollywood actors and dot.com billionaires entrusted with magically multiplying their dough. Normally people like him only showed up in the pages of *Forbes*, *Fortune*, and *The Wall Street Journal*. But he became regular fodder for magazines like *Us*, *People*, and *Tick* when he married one of his celebrity clients.

"Will Heather be there?" Lynda asked with stars in her brown and gold eyes.

"Alas, no," Mac reported. "Ms. O'Toole is shooting on location in Barbados this week, Faro informs me."

The raven-haired Irish-American beauty Heather O'Toole, who had launched her acting career with a small part in a Harry Potter movie a decade ago, was cast as the latest Bond girl in the upcoming thriller *Dragonfly*. The tabloids had a habit of referring to her by the initials HO'T, especially in headlines. I knew that from grocery shopping.

But I didn't know until later that the too-cute idea originated with Welles Faro in his *Daily Eye* column.

Lynda and Kate looked at each other. Always close, even (I found out later) when Lynda and I weren't on speaking terms, they act more like sisters than sisters-in-law. They don't even have to use words to communicate.

"You boys can go to your luncheon," Kate said. "We'll stick with the day's itinerary and go to the Tower of London for a look at the crown jewels. Lynda may even buy a few, Jeff." This was apparently a witticism aimed at my alleged cheapness. I ignored the attempted drollery.

After Mac and Kate ate, we spent the rest of the morning prowling around the Strand, Trafalgar Square, and Pall Mall. Eventually Mac and I were expected to actually work on this trip, but that wasn't on the agenda yet. I was still in honeymoon mode. And there was the rub! As noon approached and we headed back to the hotel, where Faro would pick Mac and me up, I suddenly realized that this would be the longest Lynda and I had been apart since our wedding.

"Are you sure—" I began.

"I'm sure," she said as we stood on the sidewalk outside the Charing Cross Station. She kissed me gently on the lips. "Look, I would be bored if I went along. And Mac would be lost without you if you went with me, especially if there was some crime and he had to solve it without his Watson there to take notes."

"I'm not his Watson, damn it." *Well, yes, I have written three books about his successful adventures as an amateur sleuth.*[1] *But they were my adventures, too!*

(You may wonder why I didn't say this out loud. One critic even suggested that I'm a coward because I think in italics. I prefer to believe that I'm an introvert who

---

[1] *No Police Like Holmes*, MX Publishing Co., 2011; *Holmes Sweet Holmes*, MX Publishing Co., 2012; *The 1895 Murder*, MX Publishing Co., 2012.

doesn't have to vocalize his every thought for an audience. Lynda says she likes the coward theory.)

Lynda and I parted in front of our hotel a few minutes later with a minimum of blubbering, though the rain fit my mood. She kissed me on the ear, making me tingle all over. "Have fun and don't even think about me, darling." *Fat chance.*

A short while later Welles Faro pulled up in an ancient red Ford Mondeo with the steering wheel on the wrong side.

"Hop in, gents," he said cheerfully. We did so.

Faro spoke in a slight British accent acquired from living a number of years in London—especially apparent when he broke out in Britishisms like "Brilliant!"—but he was actually an American. That seemed to give him something of a cachet in British journalism, and excused his every carefully cultivated eccentricity. He had long hair and a long beard, both streaked with gray, and a chunky build. I wasn't sure if he looked more like Walt Whitman or Karl Marx.

"You actually drive in London," I observed with a mixture of fear and admiration, holding on to the seat in front of me.

"I like the challenge," he said, looking back at me. "I've driven in Manhattan, too."

Keep your eyes on the road! The drivers in London aren't as crazy as in Rome, but they drive on the wrong side.

"It's a bit of a drive out to Berkshire," Faro said. "Hope you don't mind. This is Phillimore's country place, near Reading. Kate Middleton's parents live in Berkshire, you know."

Mac chuckled. "Well, you know what Holmes said about the country." *No, but I'm sure you're going to tell me.* He did. "'It is my belief, Watson, founded upon my experience, that the lowest and vilest alleys in London do not present a more dreadful record of sin than does the smiling and beautiful countryside.'"

That should have warned me.

By the time Mac finished the sentence, Faro was reciting it along with him.

Maybe because my father is a successful Realtor, I've always been interested in houses, so I asked about Phillimore's.

"It's a big old manor house—Headley Hall," Faro said. "I call it Deadly Hall."

"Why?" Mac asked.

"Because that's a more interesting name, don't you think? The place was in the Headley family since before the Pilgrims landed at Plymouth Rock. But taxes did them in, finally, and they sold out to Phillimore for about a million pounds. Like most billionaires, he has a bit of an edifice complex. Size matters to that sort. Nice enough chap, though."

Everything was new and interesting to me as I stared out the windows from my perch in the back seat, so the trip didn't seem too long. Gradually the rain let up and I could see the scenery better as city gave way to suburb. I suppose it was an hour and half or so before Faro pointed in the distance and said, "There it is, Headley Hall."

Well, it wasn't Downton Abbey, but it was bigger than any private residence in Erin, Ohio. Headley Hall was a stone and brick pile with a red tile roof, so Tudor in style that I almost expected Henry VIII to come swaggering out the front door munching on a turkey leg.

"How many other homes does Phillimore own?" Mac asked Faro.

"Five. Why do you ask?"

"Just to see whether you knew the answer."

The driveway was longer than Main Street in Erin. When we finally pulled up to the massive front door I was surprised there wasn't a doorman, like at a fancy hotel or a restaurant. There was a doorbell, though, and Faro rang it. I couldn't hear it ringing, so I don't know whether it belted out "Rule, Britannia!"

Have you ever seen a professional tennis player wearing a tailored suit? That's what the man who answered the door looked like. He was handsome, athletic, about six feet tall, with light brown hair and blue eyes, maybe thirty years old. His fair skin was closely shaved. He looked like a million dollars—roughly 620,000 pounds—and he made me feel like pocket change.

"Hello, Trout," Faro said familiarly.

The butler bowed the way he'd been taught in Jeeves School. "Good afternoon, Mr. Faro. Good to see you again, sir. You are expected. Please step in. Mr. Phillimore will be with you in a moment."

We stepped in. I was glad that it had stopped raining because I wouldn't want to drip on the oak floors.

I looked around the hallway, which was roughly the size of Mac's five-bedroom house, wondering whether the suit of armor came with the manor or had to be negotiated into the sale. I was pretty sure the Phillimore coat of arms framed above the archway was new—probably very new.

My gawking had gotten no further when the lord of the manor himself appeared, hand outstretched and bonhomie extended. "Faro! Good to see you! And McCabe—I have all your books! I brought that item you were so interested in." He patted his breast pocket. "Oh, this must be Thomas Jefferson Cody—love the name!"

Phillimore's high-energy performance left me exhausted, and all I had to do was shake his hand.

This whirling dervish wasn't what I had expected from the magazine and newspaper photos I'd seen where he was always wearing gray and overshadowed by some celebrity, such as his second wife. Today the only gray was in his hair and his thin mustache. He was wearing a blue blazer with brass buttons, a white polo shirt, khaki pants, and tennis shoes (which I have since learned are called trainers in jolly old England). The only thing missing was the yachtsman's hat.

Phillimore was sixty-one, making him thirty-three years older than Heather O'Toole—I'd Googled that—but he could have passed for maybe a decade younger. He was a little shorter than Trout and no more than ten pounds overweight. Phillimore was handsome, as well as fit, with a strong chin parted in the middle by a dimple.

"Ready for a spot of lunch at the Bear and Beaver?" he said.

"Right-o," I chimed in, trying to get into the spirit of the thing. "Lay on, Macduff!"

"Yes. Well. It's only a short drive."

"We can take my car," Faro offered. "It's still warmed up."

Faro got behind the wheel of the Ford while Mac and I resumed our previous posts. Phillimore was halfway into the back seat with me when he stopped. "I'd better get my brolly. Just wouldn't do to be caught in the rain without it. Won't be a moment!" He jogged back into the house.

"Nice place," I said after a while, to kill time. "I wonder if he'd sell? Lynda and I are looking to buy a place of our own eventually. We need some space for kids, lots of them. This might do."

My companions didn't respond. As the wait went on, Mac looked as if he wanted to light one of his odious cigars but was too polite to do so, or even to ask permission.

After a while, Faro looked at his watch. "It shouldn't take fifteen minutes to get an umbrella. There was an umbrella stand in the hallway, one of those horrid elephant leg things, and it was full of umbrellas."

Before Mac or I could say a word, Faro was out of the car. We were right behind him. He rang the doorbell.

Trout answered with admirable dispatch. In a clear violation of the Jeeves Code, he looked surprised.

"Yes, Mr. Faro?"

"Is something wrong, Trout?"

"Wrong, sir?"

Faro turned red behind his beard. "Yes, you heard me, damn it, I said 'wrong'!"

"What do you mean, sir?" The poor man was on the verge of stuttering.

"Mr. Phillimore came back in here fifteen minutes ago to get his umbrella and he never returned," Mac explained.

"I—I didn't realize that he'd come back, sir. He didn't call me."

Faro brushed past Trout and started calling Phillimore's name at the base of a massive staircase. Then he started poking his head into rooms, the butler at his side. This went on for maybe ten minutes or so before Faro stated the obvious:

"He just isn't here."

"It appears that he's disappeared," Mac added for good measure, "just like in the unwritten Sherlock Holmes adventure, the disappearance of Mr. James Phillimore."

Excerpt from the Professor's Journal
June 7, 2012

The game is well and truly afoot now! The first act of our little drama has gone exactly as scripted. I have no doubt that everything else will proceed according to plan. The impossible McCabe's egotistical self-assurance will be his undoing. He won't understand until the curtain falls what part he is playing.

Chapter Two
Debates

You may wonder why Lynda and I were spending any part of our honeymoon with my sister and brother-in-law. So do I. My only excuse is that it seemed a good idea at the time—not to me, but to Lynda.

Looking back, I see now that it all began when Mac wandered into my office one day three months before the wedding and announced, "I have been challenged!"

"To a duel?" I asked, not bothering to look up from working on a press release.

"To a debate!"

For Sebastian McCabe, that amounted to the same thing, for words are his weapon of choice. Mac is the author of an unconscionable number of mystery novels about a magician and amateur sleuth named Damon Devlin. He's also the Lorenzo Smythe Professor of English Literature and head of the tiny popular culture department at St. Benignus College, where I also work as the director of public relations.

I looked up. "Debate" sounded academic, which meant this might be getting into my professional orbit. "Who and what are you debating?"

Mac sat in one of my visitor chairs, a tight squeeze. "Sir Stephen Fresch, if I accept. The topic is, 'Who Was the Most Important Fictional Detective—Poe's C. Auguste Dupin or Sherlock Holmes.'"

"Wait a minute. Is this Fresch the airline guy?"

"The same."

Sir Stephen Fresch, born in Eastern Europe but now a British subject, had taken the European airline industry by storm over the past five years with a revolutionary old idea: service. His planes actually served real food and cognac in glasses made of glass. Customers willing to pay a little more for these minor luxuries after being hassled by airport security had made Fresch wealthy and knighted.

"How in the world do you know Fresch and why does he want to debate you?"

Mac waved a flipper. "I have never met Fresch, nor have I ever corresponded with him until now. I am aware, however, that he is a major Edgar Allan Poe collector and devotee, a passion that his wealth enables him to indulge to the fullest extent. We have a mutual friend and rival, Welles Faro."

That was typical. My brother-in-law always knows somebody who knows somebody. He has more than 5,000 Facebook friends, and probably just as many in real life. I've even met a few of them. Not being up on international gossip columnists, though, the Faro name meant nothing to me at the time. I said so.

"Welles Faro is an American living in London, a British tabloid phenomenon," Mac explained. "He writes a unique page-one column every day in *The Daily Eye*, mixing opinion with hard news found nowhere else. He is also a Holmesian of some stature."

This was a new one on me. "You mean a Sherlock Holmes nut? I thought you called yourselves Sherlockians."

He patiently enlightened me. "I believe it was John Bennett Shaw who said, 'In Britain the Sherlockians call themselves Holmesians, and in the United States Holmesians call themselves Sherlockians.' At any rate, Faro and I have engaged in correspondence for some years. We had a rather heated debate ourselves several months ago that spilled over into *The Baker Street Journal* in the United States and *The Sherlock Holmes Journal* in the UK."

Mac pulled out a cigar for moral support, knowing full well that if he lit it in my office I would put it out with a fire extinguisher.

"Faro wrote an intriguing but ultimately unpersuasive article contending that Holmes needed the existence of Professor Moriarty, 'the Napoleon of Crime,' to be fully Holmes. He noted that as early as *A Study in Scarlet*, the very first story, Holmes complains about the lack of a suitable adversary. Holmes found that worthy opponent only in Moriarty, of course. After the professor's demise, Holmes again bemoans how singularly dull London has become.

"Faro argued in his article, 'The Shadow of Sherlock Holmes,' that Moriarty was actually what the psychologists call Holmes's 'shadow self.' Holmes has a brother; Moriarty has a brother. Holmes has a right-hand man, Dr. Watson; Moriarty has a right-hand man, Colonel Sebastian Moran. Holmes regularly sets himself above the law; Moriarty acknowledges no law."

Being more a fan of Mike Hammer than of Sherlock Holmes, I was rather liking this theory.

"Since there was a debate, I presume you didn't agree."

Mac waved his unlit cigar. "Oh, it was a clever conceit, a kind of riff on those theories that Holmes and Moriarty were the same person." *Oh, sure.* Those *theories.* "The weakness, as I pointed out, is that many of Holmes's greatest cases took place after he dispatched the professor at the Reichenbach Falls. It's a cliché and a canard to say—as so many do, thoughtlessly—that Holmes did his best work earlier. I acknowledge the similarities between Holmes and Moriarty, two men at the top of their professions. However, to say—as Faro did—that Holmes needed Moriarty to be

Holmes simply won't wash. In the end, I am pleased to say that the greatest Sherlockians and Holmesians of the United States, Europe, and Asia took my side. It was all in good fun, of course.

"Now, Sir Stephen Fresch has invited me to engage him in a more formal debate—in person."

"Where?"

"London. I am inclined to accept. King's College would make an excellent venue."

Mac was already scheduled to be in London in June for a visit to King's College London, where St. Benignus was sending some popular culture students in an exchange program.

"I think I can do something with that," I said, thinking of a press release.

"Yes," said Mac, "I think this would be a spot of interesting publicity for St. Benignus."

That sounded innocent enough. I had no idea of the danger I was in until it was too late.

That Sunday, the subject of Mac and Kate's trip to London came up during brunch. I'd been eating with the McCabes after Mass almost every week for years. Their house is a thirty-second walk from my carriage house apartment above their garage. Now that Lynda and I were engaged, she was part of this Sunday tradition as well.

"I've been all over Europe but never to the British Isles," Lynda said conversationally.

Kate put down her fork, her green eyes shining. "You should go with us!"

I chuckled. "Too bad we already have honeymoon plans."

"But we're not going to London until a week after your wedding," Kate said, excitement building in her voice. "You could join us there after your time in Italy. You'll be so close it would be a shame not to do it. We'd have so much fun together!"

She looked at Lynda, all bright-eyed and enthusiastic. Lynda smiled back. I think that's when the deal was sealed, but at least my spouse-to-be asked me about it. "What do you think, darling?"

Hey, sure, I'd love to spend half my honeymoon with my sister and my best friend. Who wouldn't? Can you come, too, Lynda?

"Sounds expensive," I said lamely.

Lynda rolled her eyes.

"And that's a long time for me to be away from work," I added.

"Ah, but you could be working part of the time." All eyes turned to Mac. "This is a perfect opportunity for you to interview some of the St. Benignus students in our exchange program and some of the King's College teachers."

"You mean like for press releases, alumni magazine articles, blog posts, stories in the campus paper, that kind of thing?" Lynda said.

"Yep, that's what Uncle Jeff does!" Brian said. He may be eight, the youngest of the McCabe children, but he's going on sixteen or so.

"Precisely." Mac glowed. "At the very least, Jefferson, you could visit London on 'company time,' so to speak. Perhaps you could also negotiate for St. Benignus to recompense you for some of your expenses."

"With Ralph?" I gasped. "You're hallucinating."

Ralph Pendergast, who holds the purse strings to my office in his capacity as provost and vice president for academic affairs, *hates* the popular culture program. And he's none too fond of me. The chances that he would approve a farthing for a trip to London by me to promote Mac's department were about equal to my chances of winning the Ohio lottery—and I never buy a ticket.

"Wait a minute," Kate said. "Aren't you guys always complaining that when the board of trustees says jump,

Ralph asks how high on the way up?" It was a rhetorical question, so she didn't wait for an answer. "My friend Rosalie Hawthorne's father, Josiah Gamble, just got appointed to the board. I'm sure he could be helpful with Ralph."

Josiah Gamble was the current patriarch of the family that owns Gamble Bank & Trust Co. The building on campus in which Ralph's office is located was named after his great-grandfather.

So that's how, in early June, Lynda and I found ourselves flying from Venice to London on a Fresch Air flight. There had been a debate of sorts in the McCabe house that day at Sunday brunch and I had lost it.

"I wish I had one of those little foreign phrase books to translate from American to English," I told Lynda as we buckled ourselves in for the short haul. "All I know is 'What ho!' and 'Top hole, old bean!'"

"Which I'm sure you'll say at every opportunity. Don't worry, Jeff." She patted me on the arm. "You'll have Mac to translate, just like you had me in Italy."

"I'd rather have you."

And so forth.

Chapter Three
Welcome to London

We arrived in London the day after the end of Queen Elizabeth's four-day jubilee party, celebrating her remarkable sixty years on the throne. We'd watched a little of the celebrations on TV in Venice, the only place in Italy where we had a television in our room. We hadn't missed TV much in Rome and Florence, being otherwise occupied.

On the way in to our London hotel from Stansted Airport, I noticed that the remnants of the revelry had been largely cleaned up already. Union Jacks still hung from many of the shops, though. Back home I'd call them stores, but here they were shops.

Londoners must have been already thinking about their next big moment.

"Too bad we're not going to be here for the summer Olympics," I told Lynda.

She smiled knowingly. "Ha! You just want to watch the beach volleyball."

Hey, those girls are talented athletes.

"Oh, is that an Olympic sport?"

"As if you didn't know."

When we caught up to Mac and Kate at the King Charles Hotel, we found out that we already had dinner plans.

"We are dining at the Sherlock Holmes Pub," Mac announced. I could have guessed. He already owned a sweatshirt from the place.

"Cool!" Lynda said. She had developed an unexpected affection for Sherlock Holmes by reading some of the stories in Italian out of a book she bought in Rome. It would be ungracious of me to resent this, since her inexplicable fascination did help her solve a murder and a theft in the Eternal City. But that's her story, and some day she'll tell it herself.[2]

"And we shall not be alone," Mac added. "Welles Faro is meeting us there. I thought you would be intrigued to meet him, Lynda."

"Sure!"

As editorial director for Grier Ohio NewsGroup, a division of the giant Grier Media Corp., Lynda supervises and coaches news gathering for all of the company's small-town daily newspapers in Ohio. Before that, she had been news editor of *The Erin Observer & News-Ledger*. By Mac's reckoning, she and Faro were in the same field. I wasn't sure they were even playing the same game.

After lunch at a little place called Speedy's Sandwich Bar & Café and a spin around London town on a tour bus, we changed our clothes for dinner that night. Lynda looked smashing in a short, pale blue dress with a bright yellow sunflower design, which she filled out very nicely below the V-neck. Her curly, dark honey hair was pulled behind her ears to reveal blue and gold earrings. I was glad she hadn't gone Victorian on me. *Can we go back to our room now?*

The Sherlock Holmes Pub on Northumberland Street has a bustling bar on the first floor, which the English call the ground floor, and a restaurant on the second floor, which the English call the first floor. "Why can't they get

---

[2] See the bonus short story, "The Adventure of the Vatican Cameos," at the back of this book.

anything right?" I muttered as Mac explained this on the way up the stairs. Lynda rolled her eyes.

The first thing I noticed in the restaurant was a replica of the Holmes and Watson bachelor pad at 221B Baker Street. It seemed authentic enough to me, right down to the wax dummy with a bullet hole in its head from "The Adventure of the Empty House." I'd learned more than I wanted to know about that story back when Mac solved a murder among Sherlockians in Erin.

Faro was waiting for us. My first impression of the Anglo-American journalist was that Mac may have outgunned him in the pages of Sherlockian and Holmesian journals, but Faro won the beard-growing contest. It extended several inches below his chin. The hair on his head was quite a mop, too. From the salt-and-pepper color, I figured him at maybe a couple of decades older than Mac's forty.

He stood as he saw us heading his way, but not very tall. "Sebastian McCabe! We meet at last. And high time." He put out his hand for a good shake, just to prove he was still an American. "Welcome to London." The sleeves of his brown sport coat were too long for his arms.

Mac made the introductions as we positioned ourselves around the table. "I follow you daily on *The Daily Eye* website," he told Faro once that ritual was out of the way. "I think of you as a twenty-first century Langdale Pike. I mean that as a compliment."

Faro didn't look complimented.

My sister must have read the question mark on my face. "Langdale Pike was a gossip columnist who traded information with Holmes in 'The Adventure of the Three Gables,'" she explained. Kate, pulled to the dark side by my brother-in-law long ago, is a member of the Adventuresses of Sherlock Holmes.

"Gossip may be defined as idle talk or rumor," Faro said. "I deal in neither. I break more real news than any journalist in London."

"Especially since *News of the World* went down in that hacking scandal," Mac said.

"That was big news all over the world," Lynda said, "and it hasn't been all mopped up yet, has it?"

"By no means," Faro agreed. "Inquiries are ongoing. But the scandal has already cost the commissioner and one of the assistant commissioners of Scotland Yard their jobs. And it was all so bloody stupid. I didn't need to hack any phones to get where I am, just hard work. I have sources everywhere—secretaries, maids, disgruntled ex-employees, and my young Fleet Street Irregulars as well as contacts in the top of government, police, entertainment, and the arts. I get out and about all day long. I'm sure you know how it's done, Ms. Teal. Or is it Ms. Cody?"

Actually it's Teal on the job, Cody at home. But it's not my place to say so. Pretend I'm not even here.

"'Lynda' will do fine," Lynda told Faro. "And, yes, I do know how it's done. I was a working journalist before I became an editor." That used to be my gag, until it wore out its welcome. It's a load of bovine excrement, of course, because Lynda will never stop being a working journalist.

"Langdale Pike, by contrast, spent his days hanging out in the bow window of a club on St. James's Street," Mac added. "Doesn't your Binomial Theorists of London meet at a club near St. James's Street, Welles?"

Faro's eyebrows shot up. "Yes, it's Pall Mall. How did you know that?"

Mac looked like the cat that ate a cage full of canaries. "I have sources, too."

A waitress took our drink orders. Did you ever try to get caffeine-free Diet Coke at a pub in London? Don't bother. I asked for a Fuller's London Pride instead. When in London . . . They did have bourbon, but the choice was somewhat limited (one brand, and not her favorite), so Lynda ordered the house brew, Sherlock Holmes Ale.

"You're a very clever man, Professor McCabe," Faro said after some further random talk. "Almost too clever. I've read about your amateur sleuthing in Cody's books, of course. I couldn't help but think about Sir Arthur Conan Doyle, another mystery writer who was quite successful as a detective in real life. But I have to say I've been equally impressed by your literary detective work. I've been re-reading some of your Sherlockian scholarship. You did a fine job with that *Hound of the Baskervilles* controversy a decade or so ago."

Incapable of blushing or appearing modest, Mac nodded his thanks while the drinks were distributed.

"I've got to read *The Hound of the Baskervilles*," Lynda said after a long sip of her ale. "Everybody's heard of it. So what was the controversy?"

Kate jumped in. "There's always been some question as to how much of the plot and writing came from Arthur Conan Doyle and how much from his friend Bertram Fletcher Robinson," Kate said. "Remember, Holmes isn't even on the scene for a good chunk of the book. Around the turn of the current century an alleged author jumped the shark by claiming that ACD stole the plot from Robinson, committed adultery with his wife, and blackmailed her into killing Robinson."

"Good grief!" I said. "What a plot! I think I'll use it." Sometimes I forget that I don't try to write fiction anymore.

"Professor McCabe built a convincing case of circumstantial evidence that Robinson was no more than a collaborator on *The Hound*, the man who gave him the initial idea, while the writing and plot development were Conan Doyle's," Faro said.

"An English author named Paul Spiring is now the reigning expert on that subject." Mac hoisted his pint. "His researches into Robinson have far exceeded my long-ago efforts."

The waitress came and took our food orders. I opted for fish and chips, old bean. When she retreated, Faro picked up the conversation where Mac had left off.

"A friend of mine, a private collector, recently acquired an extraordinary document that settles the *Hound* controversy once and for all," he said. "It's a notebook belonging to Sir Arthur Conan Doyle. Sir Christopher Frayling owns Conan Doyle's diaries for that period, but this is something different—a small book in which he jotted down ideas for the story as they came to him. There are even places where he asks questions, noting holes that needed to be filled in later. You can see the writer at work building the story. It eliminates any doubt that Conan Doyle was the true author of *The Hound of the Baskervilles*."

"Remarkable," Mac boomed. "I would be very interested to see that!"

Mac doesn't consider himself a collector, but everybody else does. He was also responsible for getting the third largest collection of Sherlockiana in private hands donated to St. Benignus College. Murder ensued, but that's another story. The point is, artifacts interest him.

Faro sat back with a smile. "I think that can be arranged. I'll call Phillimore in the morning. That's my friend—Arthur James Phillimore."

I have a bit of a reputation, well earned, as a close man with a dollar—or a euro or a pound, for that matter. So I knew about Arthur James Phillimore, the financial whiz, from reading *The Wall Street Journal*. But it wasn't pound signs that I saw register in my spouse's eyes, it was stars. Phillimore was best known to the general public as Mr. Heather O'Toole, a.k.a. HO'T.

"How curious that a Holmesian should happen to have the name James Phillimore, even if preceded by the Arthur," Mac commented.

"The strange disappearance!" Lynda said in the same voice she used on the plane when yelling out the answer to a crossword puzzle question. Still new to Sherlock Holmes, she obviously got a kick out of picking up on the reference. "That's one of the untold tales that Dr. Watson mentions without ever telling the whole story. He says something about the strange disappearance of Mr. James Phillimore, who stepped back into his house to get his umbrella and was never seen again in this world. Even Holmes couldn't solve that one."

"As a magician, I have always had a special fascination for that untold tale," Mac said.

"It's not a coincidence that Phillimore is a Sherlock Holmes fan," Faro told Mac, without giving Lynda the verbal pat on the back that she deserved. "So many people mentioned the Holmes story to Phillimore as a young man that it drove him to the Canon."

"And to the Binomial Theorists," Mac said.

"How did you know he's a member?"

"You just told me." Mac chuckled. "Until then I was guessing. I am not above guessing, even though Holmes called it 'a shocking habit, destructive to the logical faculty.' We were talking about the Binomial Theorists right before you brought up the subject of this unique notebook. It's a natural deduction that discussing the society led you to think of Phillimore because he's a member. Besides, he's a Holmesian and a friend of yours. Why wouldn't he be a Binomial Theorist?"

This had gone far enough. I needed subtitles to follow this conversation, like when Lynda drags me to the opera, and I wasn't getting them. "Okay, I'll bite. Who are the Binomial Theorists?"

"A very exclusive society of Holmes enthusiasts," Mac said.

"No more exclusive than the Baker Street Irregulars in the States," Faro retorted, "although we are much smaller. There are just a handful of us in the Binomial Theorists of London."

"Isn't that a strange name for a Sherlock Holmes society?" Lynda asked.

"Not at all, my dear." Faro said "my dear" in an avuncular way, so I didn't have to hit him. "It refers to Professor Moriarty's most famous work, his paper on the binomial theorem, which had a European vogue. Just don't ask me what a binomial theorem is—I haven't a clue."

"At any rate, it was good of the Theorists to sponsor the pastiche contest," Mac said.

This I knew about. Mac's debate with Sir Stephen Fresch was sponsored by King's College, at Mac's request, but there was a sideshow: a contest to write the best pastiche, or imitation Sherlock Holmes story. The winner would be announced at the debate, take a bow, and collect a small library of Holmes-related books as the prize. Mac was one of the judges.

"Our pleasure," Faro said. "I'm expecting some interesting entries—but not as interesting as that ACD notebook, I'm sure. And you'll enjoy meeting Phillimore, too."

Excerpt from the Professor's Journal
June 6, 2012

McCabe has arrived in London. I didn't expect him to bring an entourage with him when I set my plan in motion. But that won't hurt anything. It just means that his wife and in-laws will watch his undoing close up. The bigger they are, the harder they fall. And he is going to fall very hard indeed.

Chapter Four
No Joke

The morning after the disappearance of Mr. (Arthur) James Phillimore, we picked up a copy of *The Daily Eye* to read Faro's account of it.

Instead of its accustomed position down the right hand side of page one, his column was splashed across the top of the page under the headline **VANISHED!** The subhead added: **Billionaire money maven walks into Deadly Hall, not seen again.** The story began like this:

> Arthur James Phillimore, investment guru to celebrities and the super-rich and slated to be named next week to the Queen's Birthday Honours List for 2012 according to Buckingham Palace sources, disappeared Thursday from his own storied residence, familiarly known as Deadly Hall.
>
> This reporter was one of three *Eye*-witnesses to the bizarre event, not counting the household staff at the Phillimore estate near Reading.
>
> Mr. Phillimore was scheduled to have lunch at his local pub, the Bear and Beaver, with the American mystery writer Sebastian McCabe; his brother-in-law, Jefferson Cody; and yours truly. He had, in fact, got into the car . . . .

I'd gotten this far when Lynda, reading over my shoulder in the hotel restaurant, snorted. "*Eye*-witness? Give me a break. That kind of breathless writing style went out with the bustle."

"You can't argue with success," I said.

"Sure I can. You just heard me."

Ignoring her, I kept reading. Faro had managed to reach Heather O'Toole—even in this story he called her HO'T after the first reference—and got a nice quote from Barbados: "Naturally I am greatly concerned about my husband and I can't imagine what happened to him. I am returning to England immediately. If the situation is as it has been described to me, I will be filing a missing persons report with the police."

"I still think it's a joke or a publicity stunt," Lynda said.

"Like Arthur James Phillimore needs publicity," I mumbled.

"And this affair has gone rather too far for a joke," Mac added, pulling up a chair. Kate was right behind him, looking bleary eyed. Her red hair was piled on top, as usual, but stray strands poked out here and there. She looked like a caffeine fiend in need of a fix.

"Don't tell me you're losing sleep over this," I told her. "Or is it jet lag?"

"It's Brian and his endless texting," she said. "As smart as he is, he can't seem to grasp the concept that nine o'clock at night in Erin is two o'clock in the morning in London."

If you'd turn off the damned smartphone, Kate, you wouldn't have that problem. I didn't say that for two reasons. The first is that people in glass houses, etc. The second is that my wife has trained me to curb my instincts to offer helpful advice. If the training hadn't worked, I'm not sure she ever would have become my wife.

Lynda passed Kate a cup of high-test coffee, which my sister grabbed as if it were a lifeline.

"So, Mac," Lynda said, "I suppose you're going to tell me you're utterly confident that Phillimore was nowhere in that house when you went back in."

"That would, perhaps, be too grandiose a claim. I have already given you my perception of what happened after we rang the doorbell the second time. I am sure you have discussed Jeff's impressions and I see that you have been reading Faro's account, which I have not read. Are there any discrepancies?"

Lynda shook her head, sending her honey-blonde curls flying. "No. There were some differences in details, but no contradictions."

With a little gentle prodding from Faro, Trout had agreed to let us split up and look all through the house. Being assured by Faro that Phillimore wasn't a practical joker kind of guy, we were concerned that the lord of the manor might be lying hurt somewhere.

Headley Hall may not be on the grand scale as far as English manor houses go, but it was plenty big for a guy who lives in a carriage house apartment. Still, it didn't take that long for the three of us to look in every room and open every closet and bathroom door. When we all assembled back in the hallway and agreed that Phillimore was nowhere to be found, Mac said, "All right, then, we shall look again, each of us taking a different room."

We kept doing that until each of us had been in every room. I guess with stealth and luck it's just barely possible that Phillimore, presuming he staged his own disappearance, might have slipped from one room to another so that he was always hiding in a room being searched by somebody who was in on the gag. But I can assure you that didn't happen.

"Magicians disappear from the stage all the time," Mac said as he dug into his breakfast. "They usually reappear in the audience. Stage magic is a very different proposition from close-up magic, however—much easier to control. Granted, I myself have performed close-up magic making small items disappear, but that—"

"Such as what?" I snapped. The lack of sleep had me irritable. It had also clouded my better judgment, which would have kept me from giving him such an opening.

"Such as your watch, old boy."

Like a chump, I pulled back the sleeve of my jacket and gave him the gaping expression he was looking for. My wrist was naked.

"Give it back, damn it."

"Of course." Mac reached into the sugar bowl and fished out my Timex. I grabbed it from him and put it in my pocket, determined to never wear a watch again. Who needs one when you have a smartphone?

The worst part of the stunt was watching Kate and Lynda trying not to smile.

"This isn't a magic trick and it isn't a joke," I said. "And considering the billions of other people's dollars and pounds and euros that Phillimore has under investment management, it's a big deal. What are you doing?"

This last was said to Lynda, who was texting away. "You've convinced me. Big deal means big story. I'm seeing if Megan wants me to cover it for Grier."

As president of Grier Ohio NewsGroup, Megan Whitlock is Lynda's hard-charging boss. She's also her mentor and chief cheerleader, having created the position of editorial director specifically to make good use of Lynda's considerable talents in reporting, writing, and social media.

"I hope you don't wake her up," I said.

"No worries. She never sleeps."

Surprisingly, Ms. Whitlock didn't text right back. We moved on to breakfast and discussion of our plans for the day.

"We have to go to Baker Street," Lynda said. "You can't go to London and not see Baker Street."

Being a good sport, I did not demur—not even silently in my head, because Lynda can hear that, too.

"Indeed not!" Mac agreed. "I have been there many times. Unfortunately, I shall be unable to join you today. Duty calls. I have to read entries in the pastiche contest. You will recall that the winner is to be announced at the debate, which is only two days away. Perhaps I will be able to join you later, if the entries are quickly dispensed with."

"Well, I'm free now," Kate said. "Let's hit the bricks before I fall asleep."

I have to admit that the apartment where Sherlock Holmes hung his deerstalker, 221B Baker Street, is one of the most famous addresses in the world. That's where we started out, sort of. You probably know more than I do about the controversy over the "real" 221B, an address that didn't exist in Holmes's day. But the Sherlock Holmes Museum claims that address, and that was good enough for my newbie Sherlockian, Lynda. For six pounds each, we got to do more than just ogle another recreation of the sitting room at 221B. We actually sat in the sitting room, imagining what it would have been like. Lynda put on a deerstalker cap provided by the museum and cajoled me into wearing a Watson-like bowler. If I ever find the photo I'll destroy it.

That was the cheap part. After a trip downstairs, to the gift shop, Lynda walked out with a shot glass for her collection, her own deerstalker cap, a ceramic Sherlock Holmes teapot, and a bag of books to add to our already over-crowded shelves.

"Do you realize how small my apartment is, Lyn?" I said. *Just asking!*

"That's why we need to buy a house, darling."

At this point I realized it would be pointless to remind her that (A) e-books are cheaper and easier to carry across oceans, and that (B) she does most of her book reading on her iPad. Holmes sickness does not bend to such rational considerations.

My sister picked up a long tie with a familiar silhouette, deerstalker and pipe, replicated dozens of times.

"Mac will never wear that," I scoffed. He sticks to bow ties, a major character defect.

"Of course not," Kate said. "I will."

I took pictures of Lynda and Kate standing in the rain in front of the museum, and then in front of the "Bar Linda" Italian café with Sherlock Holmes décor across the street at 226, and then next to a big bronze statue of You Know Who outside the Baker Street Underground Station on Marylebone Road.

Then, having no mercy on me, the women insisted that we pony up for tickets to Madame Tussauds Wax Museum just down the street. I found myself wishing I could trade those wax politicians for the real thing.

After buying some postcards to send back to my administrative assistant, Aneliese Pokorny (a.k.a Popcorn), and my favorite police chief, Oscar Hummel, we went back to the hotel to drop off our purchases. We found Mac in high good humor.

"This pastiche is a most remarkable story," he said, holding up his iPad.

"How so?" Kate asked, stifling a yawn.

"I believe it holds the secret to Phillimore's disappearance. A trip to the British Library should be sufficient to confirm my theory. Meanwhile, all of you should read it. It is rather cleverly called 'The Adventure of the Magic Umbrella.' And Arthur James Phillimore wrote it."

Chapter Five
The Adventure of the Magic Umbrella
(Part I)

"What do you know of the Paradise, Watson?"

"Very little," I replied, somewhat perplexed. "I am not a religious man, Holmes."

"Good old Watson! This Paradise is a music hall. Here, read this. It came this morning."

Sherlock Holmes reached across the breakfast table to hand me a letter along with its envelope.

It was July of 1895. We had just returned from Norway, where Holmes had concluded a matter of such delicacy that even now respect for the royal houses of Scandinavia stays my hand from recording the particulars. The letter was dated the night before.

> *The Paradise Music Hall*
> *Covent Garden*

Dear Mr. Holmes,

I am at my wit's end. Trusting in the good sense of my friend Major Pond, it is upon his advice that I wish to consult you in the most mysterious disappearance of my business partner, Mr. James Phillimore. I will present myself in your quarters at 10:05 A.M.

> Faithfully yours,
> Phineas T. Ruffle

"Well, what do you make of it, Watson?"

I held up the paper to the light, attempting to apply my friend's methods. "Strong bond and a watermark. Our prospective client is either successful in his enterprise or has another source of wealth, such as marriage or inheritance."

"Good, good. What else?"

"He is greatly upset by this matter—see how he wrote quickly, in a rather shaky hand, not even bothering to blot the ink."

"Excellent! You are scintillating this morning, Watson!"

Buoyed by this rare praise, I said, "I trust that I have deduced everything possible from this letter."

"Hardly that, my dear fellow," said Holmes. "Surely it is obvious that the writer is a left-handed retired army colonel in his late 50s or early 60s who keeps a cat?"

"Holmes!"

"You don't see a slant like that unless the writer is left handed. His age is more difficult, but I have made a special study of the effect of aging upon penmanship. I am even guilty of a small monograph upon the subject. Now consider the content of the letter. Surely only a military man used to giving orders would be so bold about setting an appointment and so precise as to the time he will arrive here. He also mentions his friend, the major. He must be of equal rank or higher. Colonel is not an unreasonable deduction."

"And the cat?"

Without a word my friend pointed to the tiny chew marks on the outside of the envelope in my hand.

"Now let's see what we can learn about our visitor from the index." Holmes pulled down from a shelf the great volume in which he had for many years docketed items of potential interest. He paged through the combination of news accounts and case notes that, in his unique filing system, he had bracketed together under the letter R. "Russian crown jewels. Red-headed League. Redstone, the blind archer. Cincinnati Red Stockings—a sporting team, mind you, Watson, not an article of clothing! Jephro Rucastle. Rembrandt Van Jones. Ah, here we are—Colonel Phineas T. Ruffle. So my inference was not so very bold after all! Served in South Africa . . . mentioned in the dispatches during the Boer rebellion of '80 . . . now co-owner of the Paradise Music Hall. But surely here is the man himself!"

Our visitor was a stout fellow, taller even than my companion, with gray hair and a walrus mustache. He strode into our room as if he owned it, clutching a top hat tightly in his right hand. His eyes darted from Sherlock Holmes to me and back again.

"Mr. Holmes?"

"I am Sherlock Holmes. This is my friend, Dr. Watson."

He pumped our hands vigorously. "Good to meet you, Mr. Holmes. Major Pond never stops talking about how you solved that rum business of the singular suicide at the Cavendish Club."

"It was a trifling affair, though not without interest," said Sherlock Holmes, but I could tell that my friend was pleased by this praise. "Someday friend Watson may wish to share an account of the matter with the public, but not until certain august personages involved have departed the stage. Please sit down and tell us your problem, Colonel Ruffle. Aside from the obvious fact that you are a widower with a young child or children and an inattentive manservant, I know very little about you."

Colonel Ruffle's eyes bulged with almost comical surprise. "How in the world—?"

"Come, come," said Holmes briskly. "When I see a man whose coat is unbrushed in a way no loving wife would ever tolerate and he is wearing a small black ribbon on the hat he carries in his hand, I should be a dull fellow indeed if I did not mark him down as a widower whose manservant nods. And when there is a bag of marbles sticking out of his coat pocket, it is no great leap to infer a child to play with them."

"Remarkable, sir! Most remarkable! Indeed, my dear wife died a year ago and I mourn her still. It may interest you to know, however, that the child in question is a cat named Freddy."

Sherlock Holmes laughed heartily, though with a rueful expression on his face. "Well, Watson, we were right about the cat, at any rate! Now, Colonel Ruffle, your story."

"And a strange story it is, Mr. Holmes."

"Leave nothing out, I beg you. We are all attention." Holmes opened his notebook and began writing.

"Well, sir, after I left the army I made my way into business. Found I had a talent for it. I dabbled in a number of different ventures, as you might call them, until I met Mr. Charles Kenworthy. He owned the Paradise Music Hall. Had a wonderful head for entertainment—he'd been a magician himself. But he was no businessman, Mr. Holmes, no businessman at all. He was losing money and needed help. I invested a goodly sum in the hall and we became partners. The Paradise was thriving when Mr. Kenworthy sickened with consumption about three years ago and died."

Holmes looked up.

"And you did not inherit his interest?"

"No, sir. His wife had died many years ago, but he had a daughter, Jane, and he left her his share. She became my partner." Colonel Ruffle shook his head. "She was clever, Mr. Holmes, I admit that. But she was a woman! I could not tolerate a woman as my partner. Could not tolerate it at all. I tried to buy her out, but she wouldn't have it and I couldn't force it. Fortunately, she married within a few months. Her husband, Mr. James Phillimore, assumed the role at the Paradise formerly held by her father. He was a bit of an odd one, but he knew the acts."

"Odd in what way?"

"He spoke very little, for one thing. And he always carried a large purple umbrella. Called it his magic umbrella. I guess it was magic at that—it made him disappear, you see."

"What!" Holmes and I interjected together.

"It happened a week ago. We were to go to a meeting together at the City and Suburban Bank on a small matter of business. I picked him up at his home, The Windings, in Surrey. He'd barely settled into the cab next to me when he suddenly became very distraught. 'Oh, drat,' he said. 'I forgot my umbrella.' 'Well, it doesn't look like rain,' I said. 'Surely you can go to the bank without it.' 'No, no,' said he, 'I must have my umbrella.' He hopped out of the cab and went into his house. I waited ten minutes, twenty minutes. Finally after half an hour I knocked on the front door. The maid answered. She said Mr. Phillimore wasn't in. That was preposterous, Mr. Holmes, preposterous! I demanded to see Mrs. Phillimore. She told me her husband had left the house half an hour before and she hadn't seen him since!"

"This is a most interesting narrative," Holmes said. "Pray continue. Obviously, Mr. Phillimore is still missing."

Our client nodded. "I went to the police right away but they said they could do nothing until he had been missing longer. Now that a week has passed they have still done nothing that I can see. I am quite lost without my partner, quite lost. Major Pond suggested that I should come to you for help in this dark matter."

"Yes, we are the court of last appeal," Holmes said dryly. "Well, let's see what we can do to shed some light. I am most anxious to see the home from which Mr. James Phillimore disappeared and to speak with his wife. How fares Mrs. Phillimore?"

"As you would imagine, she is quite worried and puzzled over her husband's disappearance."

"Doubtless. Does she know that you have come to see me? No? Well, that's no great matter. Can you go with me to Surrey, Watson?"

"Nothing would please me more, I assure you."

"Capital!"

Within the hour we were in the train to Surrey, Holmes having promised to rejoin our client later at the Paradise.

The Windings was a handsome villa in the Queen Anne style about three miles from Aldershot. The solid reality of the red brick building seemed far removed from the strange tale we had heard of the vanishing showman. We were met at the door by the maid, an Irishwoman of advanced years. She looked at us skeptically, took my companion's card, and asked us to wait in the hall. "I'll see if missus is receiving visitors," she sniffed in a thick brogue. I tried to imagine Mr. James Phillimore walking through this door to fetch his large purple umbrella and then . . . what?

We were not kept waiting long.

The woman who swept down the staircase was a tall, handsome woman with jet black hair done up in ringlets. She was solemnly dressed in a dark blue frock as if almost but not quite in mourning.

"I have heard of you, Mr. Holmes," she said without preamble. "Please tell me that you bring good news."

"I bring no news at all, madam. I have been retained to look into the disappearance of your husband."

"That is itself good news. I suppose that Colonel Ruffle hired you?"

Holmes acknowledged the accuracy of her guess. "And this is my friend, Dr. Watson. He has been of considerable help to me in my investigations."

"Yes, of course. I know his name as well. Please come and sit down."

We moved into the parlour.

"Colonel Ruffle has given us his account of the morning your husband disappeared," said Sherlock Holmes. "I should be pleased to hear what happened on this side of the door."

"There is little to tell, I'm afraid. James told me at breakfast that he and Colonel Ruffle were going to their bank to conduct some business. The colonel was to come by at nine o'clock. At the appointed hour James left and I went upstairs. That's the last I saw of him." She wiped her eyes with a lace handkerchief.

"You did not hear him return to get his umbrella?"

"No, but that is not surprising. This is a big house and I do not hear the door opening when I am upstairs in my room."

"How about the maid?"

"Annie heard nothing. I hope she wasn't too rude to you when you arrived. This was my father's house and she has been in service here most of my life. She's very devoted to me and very protective."

"May I speak with her later?"

"Of course. She has already talked to the police."

"The police!"

"Yes, I had reported James missing. An Inspector Hopkins came to make inquiries yesterday."

"I see. Our client was unaware. Well, better late than never. I'm sure we will cross paths with friend Hopkins eventually. Can you explain your husband's apparent attachment to his umbrella?"

Mrs. Phillimore smiled faintly. "His magic umbrella, as he called it? I have no idea, Mr. Holmes. He would never tell me. I believed it was some sort of superstition, perhaps a good luck charm. He took it with him everywhere."

"And yet, there it is now in the umbrella stand in the hallway. Your husband has been parted from it at last."

The missing man's wife shivered. "That is the most unsettling fact of all."

"May I look at it?"

"Please do."

Holmes fetched the large brolly and examined it closely. "Other than the fact that the owner had a small hand, a cautious nature, and medium stature, I can deduce nothing. How did you come to know your husband, Mrs. Phillimore?"

"His late father was an old friend of my father. We met when he came to offer me condolences after Father's death. He was so kind that we formed an attachment very quickly."

Holmes nodded. "I see. Do you have a photograph of Mr. Phillimore?"

"Yes, up-stairs in my room."

"Would you please bring it here so that I can see it?"

"Certainly."

As soon as she left, my friend threw himself upon the floor and pulled out a tape measure. "Watch the stairs, Watson! Let me know when she's coming back."

With amazement I saw that Holmes was measuring the floor. When he finished that he whipped out his lens and studied the point where the floor met the walls.

"Whatever are you looking for?" I asked.

"A discrepancy in room sizes that would indicate there is more to this house than meets the eye."

"A hidden room, you mean! Then you think James Phillimore engineered his own disappearance by hiding in a concealed chamber?"

"I think that is certainly a possibility," my friend said. "It wouldn't be the first time in our experience that something of the sort happened."

Before he could comment further, I alerted Holmes in an urgent whisper that Mrs. Phillimore was coming down the stairs. She entered the parlour with her hand extended, giving Holmes a cabinet-size photograph. James Phillimore was a soft-featured man with a full beard. In the photo he stood erect, umbrella in hand, wearing a bowler hat.

"Is this the only photograph of your husband?"

"Why, yes, Mr. Holmes."

"May I see your husband's room?"

"Of course." She took us up-stairs. Holmes examined every coat, shirt, tie, collar, and pair of pants in the wardrobe. He held up a collar and examined it with his pocket lens. "Glue, Watson! What do you make of that?"

"I cannot think."

"Surely that cannot be important, such a little thing," Mrs. Phillimore said.

"Oh, the little things are always the most important," Holmes said carelessly.

Chapter Six
The Brigadiers Club

That was as far I got on the first attempt at reading the short story. Kate was sleeping in her room and Lynda was on the bed surfing with her smartphone. She'd read the story first, being both more interested and a faster reader than me, while I caught up on the rest of the news in *The Daily Eye*. Miley Cyrus was getting married (who is that and why should I care?), Queen Elizabeth was all smiles after visiting Prince Philip in the hospital, and the Prime Minister was in Germany working on the European debt crisis.

After all that, "The Adventure of the Magic Umbrella" was a relief. I'd gotten about halfway through when I heard the noise from my iPhone telling me there was a text message.

How about a nap? It was from Lynda, who was lying down about nine feet away.

JEFF: *I'm not sleepy.*

LYNDA: *Neither am I, tesoro mio.*

JEFF: *Oh. Be right there!*

So I hadn't gotten any further in the story when Mac called a half-hour or so later.

"We're meeting Faro in twenty minutes at the Brigadiers Club in Pall Mall," he announced.

"And I'm sure there's a reason for that."

"Indeed there is, old boy. I need Faro's connection with Heather O'Toole to get us back into Headley Hall so I can demonstrate how Phillimore disappeared."

I sat up. "You're that sure of yourself?" *Silly question!*

"Let us say my research at the British Library proved fruitful. Meet me downstairs in the lobby as soon as you can."

"We'll be right there."

But Lynda, having heard every booming word of Mac's end of the conversation, shook her head vigorously. "Count me out, darling. I'd rather go shopping with Kate in Covent Garden when she wakes up than hang around some stodgy old club with that journalistic fossil."

"Did you hear that?" I said into the phone.

"Fossil he may be," Mac acknowledged, "but Faro knows how to fish where the fish are. He apparently spends some highly fruitful afternoons at the Brigadiers Club cultivating his sources on the upper end of the social scale."

I saw what he meant by that when we got to Pall Mall. With its marble stairs and columns, the Brigadiers Club would have looked right at home as a bank—maybe a small branch of the Federal Reserve, for example. And it wasn't the only impressive building in the neighborhood.

"Pall Mall and nearby St. James's Street are home to a great number of private clubs," Mac explained. "In fact, this area is sometimes called Clubland because the Athenaeum, the Carlton, the Travellers, the Reform Club, and so many others are located on the two streets. Mycroft Holmes belonged to the Diogenes Club here on Pall Mall. Perhaps it was this very club. By the way, I sincerely hope that dear Lynda is not upset with me for spiriting you away."

"No more than usual," I said in all truth. That's because she's never upset with him, even when I am. I don't know how he does it.

Inside the Brigadiers Club, I felt like whispering. The staircase in the central entranceway was grander than grand, the floor was inlaid marble, the carpets were out of the *Arabian Nights*, and the chandeliers hanging from the two-story ceiling could have been made out of diamonds for all I knew. So this was how the one percent lived. Not that Faro would have that kind of super wealth. But with his daily scribbling and his frequent appearances on both British and U.S. cable channels, I suspected he was more than comfortable. And besides, sometimes pounds and dollars aren't the only coin of the realm that counts. Faro had influence.

A distinguished gray-haired gentleman with the ramrod-straight bearing of royalty and a tailored blue jacket that could have been an admiral's uniform if it had the stripes, met us inside the door.

"May I help you, gentlemen?" He sounded doubtful.

"Thank you, my good man," Mac said in the same British accent he had used when playing the role of Mycroft Holmes in the play *1895* the month before. With Mac being of Irish extraction, that took a lot of McCabe-ish nerve. I was sure the accent didn't convince the major-domo of the Brigadiers Club, but he was too polite to show it. "We are here at the invitation of Mr. Welles Faro."

"Ah, yes, of course. Mr. McCabe and Mr. Cody. Mr. Faro is in the Morning Room. I'll take you to him."

We walked through the enormous foyer past marble statues of military-looking types and larger-than-life-size paintings of gentlemen who would look right at home on currency and coin of the realm. Off to one side was a long bar with a bartender on duty. The handsome wood was probably part of a tree chopped down by William the Conqueror, or maybe Richard III—one of those English guys, anyway. A quick look was enough to tell me that the array of beverages was heavy on Scotch, but Kentucky bourbon was not unknown here.

The major-domo led us into a large, rectangular room with tall windows, a grand piano, and more bookcases than the Erin public library. He faded away before I even had a chance to say, "Cheerio and all that rot!"

It must have been teatime or something because only a handful of men and women, mostly middle-aged but a few older, populated the room. We quickly spotted the shaggy-haired Faro at an oxblood leather divan, talking to another knight. Okay, I had no idea whether he was a knight, but he could have been. He was taller than me, with a high forehead and a patrician nose. We didn't meet him, not then, because he got up, shook Faro's hand, and hustled out just as we came in the room.

Faro saw us right away and waved us over.

"No problem getting here, I see. Good, good. Sit down."

"This is a most impressive office from which to gather information," Mac commented as we joined our countryman on the divan.

"Not too shabby for a poor boy from Wisconsin," Faro said. *Aw, shucks.*

"I assume this is where the Binomial Theorists of London meet."

Faro's eyes narrowed as if he were trying to figure out whether that was another guess. Then he must have remembered that he himself had told Mac they met in Pall Mall. "To what do I owe the pleasure of your company this rainy afternoon? You didn't elaborate over the phone."

"That is because I come with my metaphorical hat in hand to ask for a favor."

"Anything I can do, of course! Just name it."

"I want to get back into Headley Hall. You could accompany me, of course."

"What for?"

"To show how Phillimore disappeared."

"What? How?" Faro leaned forward, a gleam in his journalist's eyes.

Mac shook his head. "Talk is all too cheap. I would prefer to show you. That would make an excellent follow-up to today's column, would it not? I was hoping you could prevail upon Ms. O'Toole to let us return to the scene of the . . . well, I do not believe it was in itself a crime. Can you do that?"

Faro stroked his beard in a Mac-like gesture. "I think so. She was furious at me for months after I reported that her beautiful violet eyes, so frequently compared to those of Liz Taylor, came from contact lenses. But she's speaking to me again. As you saw in my column, I reached her on her cell phone in Barbados."

"How did she sound?" Mac asked. "Was she sincerely distraught?"

Faro shrugged. "She's an actress. If you're asking whether she knows what happened to Phillimore, I would love to know that myself. At any rate, I think we can get into Deadly Hall. I have to tell you, though, that we may be just one step ahead of Scotland Yard."

Mac raised an eyebrow, which was all the encouragement Faro needed to continue:

"I have just received the shocking information that my old friend Phillimore may have been running a huge Ponzi scheme, something on the order of Bernie Madoff and R. Allen Stanford. He may have bilked thousands of people out of millions of pounds. There's a Scotland Yard investigation underway right now."

"Well," said Mac, "that eliminates one mystery."

"What's that?" I said, realizing too late that's just what he wanted me to say.

"Why Arthur James Phillimore disappeared."

As we left the Brigadiers Club, I marveled aloud to Mac about Faro's sources of information.

"He must have a contact near the top of the food chain at the Yard to get the jump on a juicy story like that," I said. "Lynda will be lime green with envy."

"Near the top indeed," Mac agreed. "Did you notice the man who was just leaving as we arrived?"

"You mean the obvious millionaire or nobleman with the high forehead?"

"Actually, he is an Assistant Commissioner of the Metropolitan Police Service—Scotland Yard—in charge of specialist crime and operations."

I didn't even try to hide my surprise. "How the hell do you know that?"

Mac chuckled, damn him. "Common knowledge, old boy. Assistant Commissioner Andrew Madigan is also a member of the Binomial Theorists of London."

Faro had tried calling Heather O'Toole before we left, but no dice. I'm always amazed at how cell phones have made me available twenty-four hours a day, but not anybody else. Or so it seems sometimes. Faro promised to get back to us as soon as he heard from her.

I nagged Mac all the way back to the King Charles Hotel to tell me what he figured happened to Phillimore, but he wouldn't budge.

"Finish reading the pastiche," he insisted. "Perhaps it will suggest the answer to you as it did to me."

Chapter Seven
The Adventure of the Magic Umbrella (Part II)

After some additional little time spent exploring the missing man's room, Holmes pronounced himself satisfied. We headed back down-stairs.

"A few minutes of conversation with your maid and I shall be finished here," Holmes told Mrs. Phillimore as we descended the staircase.

"Of course. I shall send Annie to you in the parlour."

The Irishwoman joined us shortly, still displaying on her broad face an expression that if not actually hostile was certainly wary.

"You wanted to see me, Mr. Holmes," she said.

"Yes, Annie. I will only take a few minutes of your time." I was struck as I had been so often by my friend's manner of speaking up to the humble and down to the haughty. "Do I understand it correctly that you didn't see Mr. Phillimore return for his umbrella on the morning that he disappeared?"

"No, sir. I mean yes, sir, that's the way it was."

"I take it that he always carried his umbrella."

"Oh, yes," she answered hastily. "Always, sir." Apparently feeling that she was on firm ground with this subject matter, Annie's wariness disappeared.

"Well, then, do you have any idea why he forgot it that morning?"

She thought for a moment, perhaps no longer so sure of herself. "No, sir."

"He wasn't, for example, distracted or worried about something?"

"Not so's I could tell, sir."

"Thank you. I just have one more question, Annie. How did Mr. and Mrs. Phillimore get along?" He held up a hand. "Forgive my impertinence, but we are trying to find your employer."

Annie regarded Holmes sternly. "Missus is my employer, sir, just like her father before her. She and the mister were a most united couple, if you have to know. I swear they couldn't have been closer."

"And that," said Holmes in the train back to London, "was the oddest thing I heard today."

"Odd?" I repeated. "What do you mean? Surely it's perfectly natural for a husband and wife to be close." Perhaps this was something my bohemian friend with his strange humours couldn't understand. I thought back with bitter sweetness to my own all-too-brief marriage.

"It is odd," said Holmes as he lit a pipe, "because in the only photograph this woman has of her husband—the only one, mark you!—the husband is by himself, his only companion being his celebrated umbrella. Why aren't husband and wife pictured together?"

I threw up my hands in exasperation. "But surely that is a trivial matter compared to the disappearance of Mr. James Phillimore! Do you see any indications as to how he vanished?"

"There are more than just indications, surely." Holmes sat back, wreathed in pipe smoke. "I think the general outlines of the solution are in sight. What seems mysterious becomes fairly obvious when one reasons backward."

"I don't understand."

"The glue was the key, Watson, the glue! You can hardly be blamed for not seeing its significance. You couldn't know that it was the type of glue known as spirit gum, the very adhesive that I myself use to apply false beards and mustaches. So whoever wore that collar was in disguise. The implication is obvious: The man that Colonel Ruffle saw walk into this house, never to return, was in fact not Mr. James Phillimore but someone in his guise. I fear that the lovely Mrs. Phillimore is engaged in a low intrigue that required her husband's removal from the scene. *Cherchez l'homme!*"

"But the maid, Annie, assured us that the marriage was a happy one!"

"And yet there was no photograph of husband and wife together. That was suspicious from the first. No, Watson, there's another man in the case, mark my words. Annie was lying to protect her beloved mistress, to whom she is so clearly devoted. When one combines the use of theatrical makeup with the dramatic nature of the scheme, I think we shall have to look for our man no farther than the Paradise Music Hall."

We arrived in Covent Garden to find Colonel Ruffle slumped behind his desk in an attitude of defeat. When Holmes entered the room, he arose and spoke excitedly. "Thank God you are here, sir. No doubt you have solved the mystery! Is Mr. Phillimore alive?"

"I very much doubt it," Holmes said, "but I believe we at least know how he disappeared. Think back to the last time you saw him. He was only in the cab with you for a few minutes but he was somehow different, wasn't he? Perhaps you noticed a difference in his voice. Or perhaps he held his face away from you."

The big man was already shaking his head before Holmes finished the question. "No, no, there was nothing like that. I told Inspector Hopkins—"

"Hopkins was here?"

"He still is. He's talking to Masterson the Magnificent."

"Well, well, lead us to him."

Holmes had a fondness for the young inspector, who had not yet in those days achieved the fame that he enjoys today. Hopkins, for his part, held Holmes in highest esteem but also took delight in those rare occasions when he was a step ahead of the better-known private inquiry agent.

Colonel Ruffle took us to a dressing room where we found Hopkins in conversation with a young man whose image was identical to that on a poster behind him. Masterson the Magnificent was red-haired, short but powerfully built, and sported a large handlebar mustache curled on the ends.

Hopkins sprang up. "Mr. Holmes! Always glad to see you, sir!" He pumped my friend's hand vigorously. "I'm afraid you're a bit late this time, though. We already have the culprit in hand."

The other man appealed to us with a desperate look in his eye. "That's not true!" He spoke with an American accent.

"This gentleman is Mr. Grant Masterson," Hopkins went on calmly. "He's a magician. Who better to make someone disappear than a magician, eh?"

"Surely you have a better reason than that for suspecting this man," Holmes said.

Hopkins pulled out his notebook. "I have information that Mr. Masterson and Mrs. Phillimore had formed an attachment."

"Who told you that?" the magician demanded.

"I'm not at liberty to say."

"It was the Elusive Endicott, wasn't it? He's just jealous that my act is more popular than his escape routine."

"Do you deny that you and Mrs. Phillimore—"

"I deny what you're trying to imply. I am very fond of her, I'll admit that. Okay, too fond—I'll admit that, too. So I told her more than a week ago, before her husband disappeared, that she had to stop being my assistant. It wouldn't be proper, me working with her every day, feeling the way I do. She's a married woman." His hands balled into fists. "I'll make Endicott sorry that he sullied Jane's reputation!"

"Oh, Jane, is it?" Hopkins said with a leer. "And you're a bit quick with your fists, I'd say."

"How does it come to be that the wife of Mr. James Phillimore, co-owner of the Paradise Music Hall, was your assistant?" Holmes asked the magician.

"She stepped in when Lola got sick. Well, to tell you the truth, Lola's in a family way, poor girl. Mr. Phillimore heard I needed an assistant in a hurry and he said his wife could fill in. She had experience. She worked with her father in his act years ago—the Incredible Carlo. He was a good magician, though not very famous."

For a moment my friend stood silent, and then he burst out: "I've been an imbecile, Watson! I should move to the Sussex Downs and keep bees. Hopkins, you are wasting your time. I assure you that this man is innocent. Come along, Watson, we have work to do."

Leaving Hopkins, Masterson, and Colonel Ruffle gaping in our wake, we took our leave of the Paradise Music Hall. I was no less confused than that trio of gentlemen.

"But Hopkins's theory seems to be very much in line with your own," I protested as we walked out of the building. "Surely Masterson is the lover you were looking for, the man who impersonated Phillimore!"

"By no means, my dear fellow! Grant Masterson could never pose as Phillimore. His ears are all wrong. He has almost no lobes, not like Phillimore at all. You saw the photograph. Always note the ears, Watson! You can't disguise the ears with spirit gum and hair. At best, you can only conceal them. You protest? Oh, Ruffle may not have observed that, I grant you, but he could scarcely have failed to notice that Masterson had broader shoulders and shorter height than Phillimore. Now I suggest that you go back to Baker Street and await me there."

"But where are you going?"

"To Somerset House."

Knowing that it was useless to question Holmes further, and having little desire to watch the detective pour over some dusty government records, I agreed to return to Baker Street. Some hours later I was nodding over a medical journal when Holmes came into our rooms. His mood was buoyant.

"What did you find out?" I asked.

"What I expected to find out. Can you accompany me to Surrey tomorrow? Good. I am confident that a brief interview with Mrs. Phillimore will bring this matter to a successful conclusion. Meanwhile, I think supper at Simpson's would be a suitable reward for our labours."

"You have solved the crime, then?"

"There was no crime, Watson."

He would say no more on the subject, limiting his conversation over our meal that evening to the balance of power in Europe in the wake of the Bruce-Partington matter, the fifth proposition of Euclid, Verdi's *Falstaff*, and the upcoming American presidential election of 1896.

The next morning, in the train to Surrey, Holmes was scarcely more communicative.

"You mustn't be surprised at anything I say to Mrs. Phillimore, Watson," he instructed. "Our success may depend on it."

I am surprised at what Sherlock Holmes says more often than not, but I gave my word that I would try not to show it. "Stout fellow!" Holmes responded.

The maid, Annie, was in manner no less unwelcoming than on our first visit, but kept her counsel as she quickly summoned her mistress.

"What is it?" Mrs. Phillimore asked. "Has something happened?"

"There has been an arrest," Holmes said, to my unexpressed surprise. "Mr. Grant Masterson has been charged with the murder of James Phillimore."

"What!" The woman's wide brown eyes opened still wider as her delicate mouth hung open in shock. "That cannot be! This is an injustice, Mr. Holmes. You must do something!"

Holmes shook his head. "I am afraid that only you can save your noble admirer."

"What do you mean? What can I do?"

"You can tell the truth, Miss Kenworthy. There never was a James Phillimore, as attested to by the fact that there is no record of his birth or marriage at Somerset House. James Phillimore was an illusion you created with a false beard and a man's suit." My friend stepped boldly forward and lifted the woman's ringlets to expose her ears. "But the ears would have given you away. It was clever of you to hide them."

"You're the clever one," Miss Kenworthy—as I now must call her—replied. She stood taller, chin out. "You are everything I have heard about you, Mr. Holmes, including devious. Did those fools at Scotland Yard really arrest Grant, or was that a lie intended to shock the truth out of me?"

"It was a near thing, but I advised Hopkins against it."

"Then I thank you for that. I suppose you will want to hear my story. Come sit in the parlour. Does Dr. Watson take notes or does he just remember?"

"Doubtless your account will not be one I should ever forget," I said somewhat coldly.

"All right, then. My tale is really rather simple and quickly told. As you may already have learned or surmised, I grew up in the music hall. From the time I was a young girl I was assistant to my father, the Incredible Carlo. For a short while I even had my own act as a male impersonator. Oh, you found that out, too? I must say I was quite good at it and I rather enjoyed the freedom of men's clothing. When my father bought the Paradise, I saw quickly that he was not very good at business. I had some suggestions that would have helped, but he rejected them because I was a woman. We were losing money when Papa brought in a partner, Colonel Ruffle. He is a good man in most respects, but impossible when it comes to the rights of women. When Papa died, he refused to accept me as his partner and I didn't want to sell. The situation was untenable until I hit upon the happy idea of marrying. I knew of no acceptable gentleman at the time, so I invented one and announced our marriage. Colonel Ruffle was quite convinced by my male disguise. Our partnership was a happy and successful one. Notions that the Colonel would have rejected out of hand from Jane Kenworthy he accepted as genius from Mr. James Phillimore."

"Then why end the masquerade?" I burst out.

"Mr. Grant Masterson, no doubt," said Holmes.

"Exactly," Miss Kenworthy confirmed. "I grew to like him very much in a short period of time. He is intelligent, amusing, and very kind. When he expressed similar feelings for me in the most honorable way imaginable, I knew that I had found a worthy mate. But first, Mr. Phillimore would have to leave the scene. I am not sure of the law, but I know that after a certain period he would be declared legally dead and I should be free to remarry. Perhaps I erred in making his departure so dramatic. What are you going to do now, Mr. Holmes?"

Holmes turned to me. "Has any law been violated here, Watson?"

"I should think not," I said, knowing the question was a rhetorical one.

"Then I see no reason to disturb your happiness, Miss Kenworthy. Unless Hopkins errs again and imperils another innocent man, I will let the matter rest. Perhaps, Watson, it would be best if you let your readers believe this case to be another of my failures. After all, it almost was."

Thus my friend showed that he had not only a great brain but a chivalrous heart.

"This is not at all what I expected," Miss Kenworthy said with a joyful expression on her attractive features. "I am much in your debt, Mr. Holmes. How can I ever repay you?"

"You could answer a question: Why the umbrella?"

She smiled. "That was part of the magic trick—the misdirection. Mr. Phillimore's large purple umbrella was so outlandish that it is what everyone remembered about him, not his delicate features or his perhaps rather raspy voice."

It was days before I could get Holmes to discuss the adventure further one evening at Baker Street.

"There was a similar case in Manchester in '57 and another in Paris just last year," he said. "And yet I made a mistake at first by assuming that there was a real James Phillimore. When I realized that the most likely impersonator, Masterson the Magnificent, could not have undertaken the disguise, and that the putative Mrs. Phillimore was herself a child of the music hall, I began to look at things differently. The Phillimores were not in a photograph together because they were the same person, not because of some estrangement. Annie was not just her mistress's loyal servant but her accomplice. I must admit that she told the exact literal truth—a most deceptive truth—when she said that Mr. and Mrs. Phillimore couldn't have been closer!"

"But for a woman to present herself as a man for such an extended period hardly seems credible!" I protested.

"On the contrary, Watson. There have been a number of women in British history who have successfully carried out just such a masquerade for a life-time. James Barry, surgeon, and James Gray, soldier, were both women. And both named James, mark you, just like our Phillimore! Still, I take nothing away from Miss Kenworthy merely because she was far from the first. She is a remarkable woman indeed."

As Sherlock Holmes spoke, his eyes stole toward a cabinet photo on our mantelpiece and I knew that his thoughts had wandered back to another remarkable woman who had also once dressed as a man.

Chapter Eight
The Fact of Fiction

I finished reading the pastiche that afternoon sitting on the couch in Mac's suite before we went out to dinner.

"No way," I exclaimed as I put it down. "This can't be the solution to the Phillimore disappearance. I don't care how good an actress Heather O'Toole is, that wasn't her disguised as Phillimore. They don't call her HO'T for nothing!"

Before Mac could respond, our wives came into the room. They were weighed down with shopping bags, I noted gloomily. Being a good uncle, I asked Kate if she'd heard from the kids today.

"Brian is complaining that his siblings are inhibiting his self-actualization." *Well, that's what big sisters do.* "I told him I will inhibit his access to all electronic devices until he goes to college if he texts me again in the middle of the London night."

"Did you finish reading the story?" Lynda asked. "I thought it was pretty authentic, even though it was a bit shorter than the originals."

"I agree," Mac said. "It is certainly the best presented for my consideration in the contest, and quite worthy of winning. That presents something of a problem, however, with the author unavailable to claim the honor. The style of the writing is passably Watsonian, and there were quite a few touches in the storyline that ring true. For example, Holmes's first theory is wrong. That also happens in a number of canonical cases, such as 'The Adventure of the Speckled Band,' 'The Yellow Face,' 'The Man with the Twisted Lip' and even *The Hound of the Baskervilles*. One might say the plot is rather derivative, with its echoes of 'A Case of Identity' and 'The Man with the Twisted Lip,' but that, too, is canonical. Several of the later Holmes stories have plot lines similar to the earlier ones.

"The reference to other cases is classic Watson. I blush to note that the allusion to 'the singular suicide' at the Cavendish Club is clearly a nod to my own mystery novel, *Nothing Up My Sleeve*, in which 'The Singular Suicide' is a chapter title. You will recall that in that book Damon Devlin solves a murder made to look like a suicide made to look like a murder."

No wonder I don't read your books more than once, and that just for friendship.

"If the author was trying to curry favor with one of the judges, it worked," Mac droned on. "I also found the references to misdirection—"

"This is a fascinating exercise in literary criticism," I lied. "But I repeat: You can't expect me to believe that Phillimore was really his wife in disguise."

"Indeed I do not!" Mac said, as if the mere idea was the most ridiculous notion in the world—which, of course, it was.

"But you said the solution was in the story!" I sputtered.

"And so it is—not in the solution of the story, but in a possibility that Holmes investigated and rejected."

"A hidden room!" Lynda said.

"You mean like in *Scooby-Doo*?" I said acidly. "Oh, come on. That house has been standing like that for hundreds of years."

Mac nodded. "Just so—it has been standing like that with a hidden room. Or, to be more precise, it has a priest hole. I am a dolt for not exploring that possibility last night."

I was tired of staring blankly at Mac, so I turned to Lynda . . . and stared blankly at her.

"Weren't priest holes where Catholic priests hid during the time of the persecutions?" she asked my brother-in-law.

"Precisely," Mac confirmed. "Altar vessels were concealed there as well. Priests in those days, the sixteenth through eighteenth centuries, were forbidden by English law from celebrating the Mass. The penalties escalated up to life in prison for a third offence. In practice, some priests were tortured—usually drawn and quartered—and then executed. Nevertheless, many wealthy Catholics had priest holes concealed in their homes. St. Nicholas Owen, a Jesuit lay brother, was quite skilled at building and concealing them. He was caught and tortured to death on the rack.

"In a sense, priest holes were not all that different from the secret room in my home and others on the Underground Railroad used to hide runaway slaves on their way north to Canada and freedom. Berkshire, where Headley Hall is located, was particularly known for having numerous priest holes in the homes of the local gentry."

"And you know this how?" Kate demanded before I could.

Mac shrugged his massive shoulders. "I must have read it somewhere, possibly while researching something else. You know how the McCabe mind works, my dear: What I read, I seldom forget. Where I read it, I seldom remember. I must shamefacedly admit that the notion of a priest hole as a hiding place for Phillimore did not occur to me until I read the pastiche with Holmes looking for a secret room. Then it struck me like a body blow. I was able to confirm at the British Library not only that the Headley family was Catholic, but that there were rumors of a priest hole on the premises."

Being a neophyte Catholic, this idea of throwing Jesuits on the rack was all new to me, but I didn't interrupt with questions. Mac assured me later that English Catholics started getting legal rights at the end of the eighteenth century. Flash forward to 1994 and a member of the royal family, the Duchess of Kent, became Catholic with scarcely an eyebrow raised. Today, the monarch can even marry a Catholic. Sometimes change is a good thing, although you should never bet on it.

"When Holmes looks for a hidden room in 'The Adventure of the Magic Umbrella' and says 'it's been done before,' that is a clear reference to two Holmes stories with a hidden room—'The Adventure of the Norwood Builder' and *The Valley of Fear*," Mac said. "Both of those cases took place before the 1895 setting of this story. To me, however, it seemed like a neon sign pointing to the present whereabouts of Mr. James Phillimore."

This didn't track for me. "Are you saying that Phillimore wrote into this story a clue to how he disappeared? But why do that if his goal was to slip out of Dodge before he could get arrested? In fact, why stage such an elaborate, attention-getting disappearance to begin with?"

"What!" Lynda said. "Arrested? I think I must have missed a chapter." She looked from me to Mac to me again. "Would you boys care to fill me in?"

Oops. With all the chatter about the pastiche, we hadn't gotten around to debriefing our wives about our discussion with Faro. Mac brought them current with the news that Phillimore apparently had been running a giant Ponzi scheme.

"Hot damn!" Lynda responded. "The story gets even bigger. And I got a text from Megan while we were at Covent Garden—she wants me to pursue it, all right." She chewed a nail. "But I'll never catch up to Faro and all his sources. I have to find a unique angle."

"You can go with us on our return trip to Headley Hall," I said.

"So can Faro!"

"But you have special access to the genius who figured it out." I turned to Mac. "Presuming you did figure it out. You'd better be right. And you still didn't answer my questions about why he'd disappear in such a pulp novel way and why he'd leave a clue, if he really did and it's not just your imagination."

Mac put on that Mona Lisa smile that drives me nuts. "I am not certain that the clue was deliberate. Perhaps it was subconscious. Perhaps the fact that the notion of a hidden room proved to be a dead end in the story was intended to throw us off the trail. That remains to be seen. I have not solved all of the mysteries yet, old boy. Give me time."

Excerpt from the Professor's Journal
June 8, 2012

Phillimore suspects something. "I read suspicion in his eyes," as Porlock wrote to Sherlock Holmes. He has proved more astute than I expected. But it's too late for him now. He's cowering away in his luxurious hideout, totally dependent on me. Unfortunately, as he is beginning to fear, he made the mistake of putting himself into the wrong hands. He probably worries that I am going to turn him in to Scotland Yard. He should be so lucky.

Chapter Nine
The Ponzi Principle

"What are you doing?" I asked Lynda.

"Writing on my iPad."

Patience, Jeff. "I can see that, my lovely wench. *What* are you writing on your iPad?"

"Call me that again and I'll give you a free taekwondo demonstration. You won't like it." *What, you don't like being called lovely?* "I'm brainstorming ways to get into the story with a different angle."

Welles Faro, as expected, had broken the story of Scotland Yard's investigation of Arthur James Phillimore with another huge top-of-page-one column in *The Daily Eye.* The other London papers, meanwhile, were absorbed with comparatively trivial matters like the torrential rains battering the British Isles, Prince Philip's continuing hospitalization, and the Euro 2012 football (a.k.a. soccer) tournament which had opened the day before in Warsaw with a 1-1 tie between Greece and Poland.

"But we're on our honeymoon!" I protested.

"Honeymoon, yes. Vacation no. And aren't you supposed to be working, too?"

Oh, that. It was Saturday morning, before breakfast. We'd been in London since Wednesday. Although Mac had already done some of his business at King's College before we arrived, and was going to go back, I hadn't yet made that trek. We'd been busy with other things. Eventually we would have to justify the deal I had struck whereby I was considered to be on the clock for St. Benignus part of the time in London because I would be working up publicity on the exchange program.

"I'll get around to it," I promised.

It wasn't that I hadn't been thinking of the college. In fact, I missed the campus, as well as Erin, my nieces and nephews, Popcorn, and even Oscar. I liked to travel, but it seemed that we'd been away so long. Well, it didn't help any to dwell on that. I tried to scrunch up my homesickness into a little ball and shove it to the back of my mind. At least the love of my life was with me.

"So what's on your to-do list today?" I asked.

"First," Lynda said, "I need to get an interview with that Assistant Commissioner, Andrew Madigan. He's the wheel behind the investigation."

"That sounds like a conflict of interests, or at least an oddity. Madigan and Phillimore, if not friends, are at least more than nodding acquaintances. They're both members of the Binomial Theorists."

"Good point." She typed. "I'll ask him about that. I also have to find out more about how this fraud worked. Faro's breathless column this morning was heavy on shock and pretty skimpy on facts."

"Faro said it was a Ponzi scheme. The Ponzi principle is simple enough." Knowing that I pay attention to this stuff, Lynda was all ears. Wait, scratch that. Sitting on our bed in her yellow satin pajamas, bent forward to type on the iPad on her lap, it was obvious that she was *not* all ears. But she was paying attention to what I was saying. I diverted my eyes from her shapely body so that I could pay attention to what I was saying, too.

"A Ponzi scheme is a fraudulent investment scam in which existing investors are paid out of money coming in from new fish entering the pipeline. Even though the investors are getting a huge return on their money, the scammer is getting even more. And eventually it all collapses because there aren't enough new investors to keep it going forever. I think most of the time the legal authorities step in before it gets to that point. If it gets big enough that hundreds of investors are involved, eventually somebody smells a rat."

"And why is it called a Ponzi scheme?"

"It was named after one of your countrymen, an Italian immigrant named Carlo or Charles Ponzi. He worked a scheme like this in the early 1920s in Boston. But the idea was around long before him, and keeps getting resurrected for new generations of suckers."

"Wasn't that Madoff business a Ponzi scheme?"

I nodded. "The biggest of them all, so far. It all came unraveled at the end of 2008, during the Great Recession, when a lot of his clients panicked and wanted to cash out. That's when they found out there wasn't any cash and their investments were essentially worthless. I don't know how many thousands of investors Bernie Madoff bilked, but I know they ranged from well-heeled individuals to big-name charities."

"I followed it at the time, but I'm sure not as closely as you. How much money was involved?"

Numbers are not her strong suit. "That's hard to say. Some of the early estimates were as high as $65 billion missing from client accounts, but—"

"Billion?" Lynda's eyes widened.

"With a 'b.' But that figure was probably too high because it included a lot of investment gains that never really existed and therefore wasn't actually money lost. I think the bean counters figured out that Bernie Madoff and his associates actually stole somewhere between ten and eighteen billion. Whatever the real number was, it got Bernie a hundred and fifty years in federal prison.

"Next up among the big Ponzi schemers was a guy named R. Allen Stanford. He was convicted a few months ago in Texas of bilking investors out of more than $7 billion. I think he's going to be sentenced later this month."

"How do you remember all that stuff, Jeff?"

"I'm very good with numbers"—*yours are 38-28-38!*—"and I've always been interested in investments."

"So when's my birthday?"

"December first." *Good thing I remembered that number!* "You'll be thirty-one."

She didn't linger on that topic. "Why do people fall for these scams and schemes?"

I smiled ruefully. "The idea of wealth without work or risk never seems to lose its appeal. When the stock market is down, as it was at the end of the last decade, and interest rates on CDs are in the low single digits, I guess it's hard to remember the old rule that if it seems too good to be true it probably is."

She regarded me shrewdly. "I've been following your advice on my 401(k) for years, Jeff. I hope you haven't—"

I protested with my hands. "Not to worry! Don't you remember? You were going to put it all into Grier Media Corp. stock, but I talked you into a prudently diversified portfolio of stock and bond mutual funds which I rebalance periodically in light of your projected retirement date."

"Whatever that means," she muttered, going back to her typing.

Financial planning and saving are not Lynda's strong suits. She does fairly well at spending, though.

I was about to explain to her that, thanks to my wise advice, her retirement portfolio was growing nicely when I heard a rap at the door. I looked through the eye-hole. My brother-in-law was standing in the hallway, filling up the view available through the wide-angle lens.

"It's Mac," I reported to Lynda. "You'd better get decent."

"I'm always decent, darling. I'll put on a robe." Marry a wordsmith and that's what your conversations are apt to be like.

When I let Mac in, he gave evidence of being under the influence—of caffeine.

"Good news, Jefferson!" he boomed. "Ms. O'Toole has granted us an audience at Deadly Hall."

"Don't call it that," I said. "That name gives me the creeps."

"Besides," Lynda added, tying the belt around her robe, "it's a Faro-ism." *Are you saying he's not your favorite Anglo-American journalist covering this story?*

Mac bowed graciously. "As you wish."

He thought we could get a start on planning the day while Kate was finishing her shower. Heather O'Toole was expecting us around noon.

"When are we going to King's College?" I asked. "We're actually supposed to be working on this trip, remember?"

Mac waxed indignant. "I assure you that thoughts of my beloved popular culture program have never been far from my mind. Tomorrow night, before the debate on the King's College London campus, we are dining at Simpson's in the Strand with Professor Ralston as well as Sir Stephen Fresch." Althea Ralston, no doubt some dry-as-dust academic, was the moderator of the debate as well as Mac's principal connection on the KC campus. "I also have an appointment with her on Monday, at which time you will accompany me and photograph the campus, interview her, etc. —whatever it is you do."

"And he does it very well," Lynda said stoutly.

We decided that today was to be our museum day, so we spent the morning at the fabulous British Museum. It was hardly spoiled at all by Mac's lectures on the way.

"Holmes once had rooms just around the corner from the Museum on Montague Street," he informed us as we set off.

"Didn't that guy in the 'Blue Carbuncle' hang out at the British Museum?" Lynda asked.

"Indeed he did," Mac confirmed, "and at the nearby Alpha Inn, which most scholars believe is actually . . ."

And so forth. By the time we got there, Mac had discussed in excruciating detail how the British Museum is mentioned in five Sherlock Holmes adventures.

Looking like a Greek temple, Britain's national museum is one of the world's greatest collections of, well, everything—about eight million permanent items, according to the guidebook I flipped through. One of the special exhibits was on Shakespeare. We practically had to pull Mac away from it to get to Headley Hall by noon. He thinks he's Falstaff.

The logistics of getting there had been worked out in the morning, but it wasn't easy. Lynda initially balked at Faro's offer to drive us.

"I hate being dependent on that throwback to the Brass Age of journalism," she sulked.

"I can understand that," Kate said.

"Sure." I nodded. "I'm simpatico, too, but let's face the facts: If it weren't for Faro, we wouldn't be getting into Headley Hall at all."

Lynda rolled her eyes. "I wonder what his angle is. He's not helping us out of the goodness of his heart."

"Perhaps"—Mac added that word at the beginning of the sentence just to appear modest—"Faro would like to see Sebastian McCabe in action."

Kate insisted that she had no desire to go along. "I have to catch up on some long-distance mothering," she said grimly, holding up her smartphone.

I had a feeling some virtual fireworks were on her agenda.

Chapter Ten
HO'T Time at Deadly Hall

Except for the fact that Lynda was sitting in the back seat of Faro's Ford Mondeo with me, holding my hand, our arrival at Headley Hall was like a rerun of two days before. It was still raining.

This time, though, the massive front door opened before we even got out of the car. A man with shoulder-length hair in a ponytail came out, paused, and opened an umbrella. Beneath his Chicago Bears T-shirt lay a powerful physique. Behind him I spotted Trout, the Phillimore butler, standing in the doorway. Trout watched the bruiser for a moment, as if to be sure he was really leaving, and then shut the door.

"That's Rod Chance!" Lynda exclaimed. *Why don't you yell in my other ear and make them even?*

"I'll have to trust you on that."

Lynda is a lot more up on sports than I am, except for Cincinnati Reds baseball. But even I'd heard of Rod Chance. Until being sidelined by a leg injury earlier this year, he was known around the world as the bad boy of soccer—or football, as they call it on the British side of the pond. A South African playing for a British team, he was known for his violent temper and the huge multi-year contract he had signed five years ago. His career had already been on the decline before the injury, creating fan resentment and leading to tabloid headlines like **NOT A CHANCE**.

Potentially a has-been at age thirty-two, Rod Chance also had one other claim to fame: He was the first Mr. Heather O'Toole, the man she'd divorced to marry the even-richer Phillimore. They'd had some famous late-night rows when they were married. But now we'd just seen him leave the house her current husband had disappeared from. If I were the suspicious sort . . . Actually, I *am* the suspicious sort. I'm also the new son-in-law of two people who had remained romantically linked, off-and-on, for decades after their divorce. The existence of Lynda's younger sister, Emma Teal, was living proof of that.

While I was musing along these lines, the athlete hustled down the drive and hopped in a late-model silver Jaguar with the license plate HOT ROD 1.

"Taking notes, Mr. Faro?" Lynda asked archly.

"No need to, my dear." The columnist smiled and tapped his forehead. "It's all stored up here."

He parked the car.

If I'd entertained any thoughts that Trout would welcome us as old buddies, they died a quick death when he opened the door. He was friendly, as before, but in a reserved British way. After telling us that Ms. O'Toole would be right with us, he retreated into the back of the house.

We waited in the massive entranceway. Lynda smoothed her dress, a luscious chocolate and gold number she had bought at some horrendously expensive shop in the Via Condotti in Rome as a honeymoon indulgence. I usually shop for clothes at the St. Vincent de Paul Store in Erin.

"It's hard to believe I'm in the home of Heather O'Toole," Lynda said, her professional reserve totally MIA.

Have you ever met somebody in person that you'd previously seen only on television or even on the big screen? They're usually shorter, or fatter, or have more wrinkles, or are disappointing in some other way. In Heather O'Toole's case, the main difference was that she seemed more human than in the movies. She bounded down the staircase—no grand entrance for her—wearing jeans and a man's white shirt with the sleeves rolled up to show muscular arms. Her thin sandals and her toenails were the same shade of gold. She wasn't built like Lynda, but nobody would mistake her for a boy, either.

Her wavy black hair hung shoulder length, just like her ex-husband's. But she was better looking, with creamy skin, full red lips, and wide eyes. I wondered whether the long dark lashes were as phony as the violet of those eyes, but only for a moment. That's all it took for me to decide it didn't matter. She was somewhere north of very pretty and only slightly south of beautiful, which is a very nice neighborhood to hang out in. It wasn't hard to see why she'd been cast as the newest Bond girl in *Dragonfly*. But in manner, she was more like the friendly, volleyball-playing girl next door (assuming you didn't live next to Wendy Kotzwinkle, who threw me over for that football player in the eleventh grade).

"Hello, Welles, always good to see you," she tossed off. She didn't mean it, and she didn't bother to act as if she did. Her voice reminded me that she was an American. That was easy to forget because most of her films from Harry Potter on had her speaking in a British accent.

Heather put out her hand and shook each of ours in turn as Faro made the introductions. (I'm sure the girl next door wouldn't mind if I called her Heather.) It was a firm handshake, and I thought that James Bond had better watch out. Even in sandals she was taller than Faro. I caught a whiff of the intoxicating Birth of Venus perfume, lightly applied.

"I suppose you've heard nothing new about James?" Faro said.

She shook her head. "Only what I read in your column this morning. That was all totally new to me. This whole crazy-ass situation is devastating, Welles. First he disappears, and now I find out he's some kind of crook."

"We are sorry to intrude on you at this difficult time," Mac said. "I hope that this is no more inconvenient than necessary. We noticed another caller leaving. If our visit was the reason . . ."

Heather waved the notion away with a swat of her hand. "That was just Rod, my ex. He's one of my husband's unhappy investors. As usual, he threw a temper tantrum like a two-year-old. I had to have Trout throw him out."

Mac raised an eyebrow. "And that worked?"

"Maybe you didn't notice, but Trout has muscles to spare." Actually, I *had* noticed. "He isn't just a butler; he's also my personal trainer and bodyguard when I'm home. I may need more bodyguards to fend off Phillimore investors as the bad news spreads. There must be thousands of us."

"Us?" I blurted out.

"Yes, I'm one, too, damn it. I was James's client before I became his wife. Right now I'm feeling pretty foolish about being either one. Rod thinks I knew something about this fraud business, but I didn't. I'm a babe in the woods about money stuff." *You're a babe, all right!*

My favorite journalist looked skeptical. "Didn't you graduate *summa cum laude* from Vassar?"

"I majored in history, not finance."

"But wasn't your father something on Wall Street?" Lynda persisted.

Heather's smile was hard to read. "You seem to be an expert on me, Ms. Teal-Cody." That's how Faro had chosen to introduce her. Although it's not Lynda's preferred moniker, she offered no correction.

"I read a lot," Lynda said.

"Well, I hope you don't believe everything you read. You know how journalists are."

Can we change the subject now?

I don't know whether Mac noticed that Lynda was fuming, any more than I know whether HO'T intended her comment as a slap at Faro, or Lynda, or both. I don't even know if she was aware of my wife's profession. At any rate, Mac spoke up.

"Ms. O'Toole, I am sure you know we came here on a mission," he said.

"I just know that Welles said you have some notion about a hidden room in the house. Where did you get that silly idea?"

"From a short story your husband wrote."

"A short story? James? I didn't know he could write anything except checks." *I bet.* "Welles also said something about hiding priests." Heather shook her gorgeous head skeptically. "I don't think James was hiding any priests."

"Perhaps not," Mac said, as if making a big concession. "It is, however, more than possible that the original owners of the manor may have done so. That is why we were hoping to get your permission to search for a secret room in the house."

"I've already given it," Heather said. "That's why you're here. Go ahead and look. Just don't get sticky fingers. And if you find James"—she gave an ironic smile that I bet she had practiced in the mirror—"tell him to have his lawyer call my lawyer. If you need anything, Trout will be around somewhere. I'll be upstairs working on my lines."

For the movie, or for your interview with Scotland Yard? As I said, I have a suspicious mind.

"So what are we looking for?" Lynda asked after Heather had gone back upstairs.

"Anything that does not look like the entrance to a secret passage," Mac said. *In other words, you haven't the foggiest.* "Priest holes were made by carpenters, so look at the wood very closely. Stairs and paneling were common places for concealed entrances. There were also a few instances of false fireplaces. Most often the priest holes themselves were in basement or attic areas. My conjecture is that somewhere on this floor is an entrance to a hiding place underground. Trout said that he was upstairs the other night and did not hear Phillimore return after he left with us, so it is likely that he did not go above the ground floor."

"I'll take the library," Faro said.

Mac claimed the dining room—his favorite room in any house, next to whichever one has the most books— while Lynda and I went to the parlor together. I insisted that we would act as a team, the honeymooners.

"What do you think?" I asked her when we were alone. "Is this whole idea totally nuts—or just slightly?"

"That depends on whether we find a hidey hole. Get to work."

Lynda started at one end of the room while I attacked the other. Mac's instructions to examine the wood gave us plenty to work with because there was a wainscoting that went up about three feet all around the room. Wherever there seemed to be any kind of seam or joint, I pushed, pressed, and pulled, trying to find an opening. What it would open *to*, I had no idea. What was on the other side of the parlor? In a house this big, it was hard to tell. "A map would help," I muttered.

After about ten minutes of fruitless peering and poking, Lynda said from the other side of the room, "So, do you think she's pretty?" *Uh-oh. Incoming! Incoming! Step carefully, Jeff!*

I gave that a think before I said, "Oh, you mean Heather O'Toole? I didn't notice."

I wasn't looking, but I could hear Lynda roll her eyes. "Is that the first lie you've told me since we've been married, Jeff?" *And when did you stop beating your wife?*

"That's a very good question. You should be a reporter." I chuckled. "Of course, she's very beautiful for a famous movie star." *Wait, that didn't come out right. Can we open some windows?* "But, you know, beauty is only skin deep." *Of course, plenty of guys would like to go skin diving with her!*

Lynda sighed. "And she's wearing my mother's favorite perfume, too. The one she's famous for."

Of all the women in the world, Lynda's mother was the last one Lynda wanted to be reminded of. And that goes double for me.

"Do you think we're finished here?" I asked.

"Well, we've each been over the whole room twice without finding anything, so I guess so."

We ran into Mac in the hallway. "Any luck?" I asked. He shook his head grimly. "Perhaps Faro . . ."

But we found Faro sitting on a window seat, reading a book. This wasn't the sort of library with shelves floor to ceiling on all four walls. It was a big, open room with several bookcases with glass doors, a globe, and assorted chairs and love seats.

"Really, Welles," Mac boomed, "this is no time to pursue your literary interests."

Faro held up the book so that we could see the title, *Priest Holes of Berkshire*. "I'm researching. Haven't found anything useful yet, though."

"You're supposed to be searching, not researching," Lynda snapped.

"Already have," Faro drawled. "Following Professor McCabe's instructions, I looked particularly closely at the paneling and the fireplace. I also examined the bookcases for that old canard of the bookcase that swings out like a door. Nothing." He closed the book and made a show of looking around. "Have I missed anything?"

"I suppose not," Mac growled. "I assume the window seat is solid?"

"Oh!" Faro stood up as if his pants were on fire. "When I was checking out one of the bookcases I saw this book and sat down to read it. I haven't looked inside the window seat."

"It looks like it could be original to the house," Lynda said.

I think she meant that it was no stretch to assume that the wood was milled more than five hundred years ago and then fashioned into a window seat about six feet wide and maybe two feet deep.

Like many window seats, the top opened on hinges like a lid—not the entire top, but the middle portion. Faro opened it and removed some blankets from the floor. Kneeling, he reached down and tapped the bottom. "Seems solid. But look"—he pointed and his voice rose in excitement—"it should be bigger on the inside. I think the third section, the farthest to the right, is gimmicked."

Mac moved to the right end of the window seat before Faro could stand up. "I read about a priest hole entrance through a window seat. I should have thought of it earlier."

He pushed here and he pushed there until he must have hit on a hidden spring. That third of the window seat slid to the left, revealing a gaping darkness.

"Holy shit," Lynda breathed.

Mac struck a match and gave it to Lynda. She knelt down, a maneuver my brother-in-law was not built to execute with any great agility, and held the match into the mouth of the darkness.

"There's a ladder," she said. "I'm going down it."

"Then so am I," I said. *I guess it would be pointless to point out that you might get your expensive new dress dirty.*

"Okay, but Mac and Welles, you won't fit. The opening is too narrow."

Mac handed her a pack of matches, which wouldn't have been necessary in her smoking days. "You will need more."

I won't pretend the few seconds it took us to climb down that ladder backwards didn't creep me out. The light of the match cast weird, flickering shadows and I didn't know what we were going to find down there. A dead body wouldn't have surprised me at all. But instead we found . . .

An uninhabited room. It was ten feet by ten feet square and not much more than seven feet high. It made me claustrophobic, especially the height, but people were a lot shorter when it was built. It was sparsely furnished with a camp bed and a wooden chair, old but not sixteenth century. A battery-powered lantern sat on a small table.

"This wasn't left by a priest in hiding a few centuries back," I said, picking it up.

"Neither was this." Lynda held up two wrappers from Cadbury Dairy Milk candy bars. *Wanted: One fugitive felon with a sweet tooth.*

"What do you see down there?" Mac called.

"Phillimore's not here," I said, "but he was."

"Take pictures with your iPhone, please." It annoyed me that Mac thought I wouldn't think of that. It annoyed me even more that I hadn't thought of that. But Lynda was already snapping away.

"I wonder why he didn't suffocate," I said.

"He wasn't here that long," Lynda said. "Besides, if you look up in the corner of the ceiling you'll see little air holes."

Within ten minutes we were back up in the library. Lynda's dress was soiled, but nothing permanent. I was sure she wouldn't care anyway. She had a hell of a story to write.

"The big question," she said in the car on the way back to our hotel, "is how and when he emerged from hiding and got away."

Mac waved that away as trivial. "Obviously he had an accomplice who helped him escape later. Whoever it was replaced the blankets and closed the window seat so that we saw nothing amiss when we searched the first time. Other than Phillimore himself, that co-conspirator is probably the only one who can answer the really big question:

"Where is Arthur James Phillimore now?"

Excerpt from the Professor's Journal
June 9, 2012

McCabe is acting exactly as I had expected. I should feel triumphant, vindicated that I read him so well. Alas, I'm actually rather disappointed. Where is the challenge in a game with no surprises? Who would go to a sporting event if you knew exactly what was going to happen in every period? Well, perhaps Act II of our little drama—to mix metaphors—will add a dash of the unanticipated.

Chapter Eleven
Simpson's in the Strand

Lynda pulled the iPad out of her purse and started writing her story while we were still in the car. Almost certainly Lynda's boss, Megan Whitlock, would send it on to Grier News Service, which serves the whole Grier newspaper chain plus dozens of other papers that use it as a supplementary wire to the Associated Press.

Faro watched Lynda in the rearview mirror as he drove. If he was chagrinned that she was going to score an international scoop, he had the grace not to show it. Whatever his story lacked in exclusivity, it made up for in color. The headline on his column splashed across the front of *The Daily Eye* the next day read **BILLIONAIRE'S BIZARRE BOLT HOLE**.

"Mine reads more like a news story, not a graphic novel," Lynda sniffed over breakfast. "Megan texted me that it was picked up by a lot of papers."

Faro's florid account of yesterday's adventures was accompanied by two uncredited photos which Lynda took, at Faro's request, using his camera. Fair is fair, and Lynda had to admit that she wouldn't have even been there without his intervention with Heather O'Toole, not to mention his driving us to the house.

Heather's reaction to events seemed to be a mixture of surprise that there really was a secret room at Headley Hall and outrage at this confirmation that her husband had done a bunk. "If he's hiding out on a South Seas island with some other woman and never gets found, I'll kill him," she said. My mind was still trying to process that illogical rant when she left to call her lawyer. Now that it was clear that her husband was on the run, she was worried about her legal standing with regard to the fraud and the O'Toole-Phillimore family assets that might get attached to reimburse investors. To me this mess was already looking like a lawyer full-employment plan.

After eating another cholesterol-loaded breakfast, we went with the McCabes to Westminster Cathedral for Sunday Mass. Not to be confused with the more famous Westminster Abbey, which is Anglican, the Cathedral is the mother church of English and Welsh Catholics. It's a brick and stone building in neo-Byzantine style, not much more than a hundred years old.

Lynda wore the cameo necklace that I had bought her at the Vatican, which had been stolen in Rome but recovered.

As we were leaving the Cathedral, Lynda pulled out her smartphone and emitted a cry of surprise. "Faro wants to be my Facebook friend! What should I do?"

"Keep your friends close and your enemies closer," I said, not claiming any points for originality. "Maybe he'll post something indiscreet on his status and you'll get a leg up."

She Friended him.

After lunch, we visited the National Gallery, right near our hotel on Trafalgar Square. We saw so many paintings by Italian artists that we could have been back in Rome or Florence. Kate was in her element, often telling a racy anecdote about the artist or calling our attention to a master stroke that made a painting genius and not just a nice picture. But I could tell Lynda's mind was elsewhere, churning over the next stories to be researched and written.

She dressed in red that night for dinner at Simpson's in the Strand and the debate at King's College. Lynda's favorite colors are the bright yellow of her Mustang—which she drives too fast—and red. I've noticed that she wears red when she wants to make a splash or when she's in a particularly buoyant mood. And it looks great on her. Tonight she donned a scarlet skirt, a frilly white blouse displaying her generous bosom to good advantage, and a mostly-red Pashmina scarf that she had bought at the market in Florence. She picked up the same color theme on her toes and lips.

She stood in front of me in our room and pinned on the scarf a colorful enamel pin of a parrot that I had bought her a couple of weeks before the wedding. "How do I look?"

"The expression 'woo-woo' comes to mind."

I moved closer. The smell of Cleopatra VII, Lynda's favorite scent, filled my nostrils.

"Down, boy. Don't mess up my hair, smear my lipstick, or disarrange my scarf." *Other than that, have your way with me!*

Seeing the pout on my face, Lynda smiled. "I have to give you something to look forward to, don't I?"

I couldn't argue with that. After dinner with some fussbudget professor and the owner of Fresch Airlines, followed by a debate over the oh-so-gripping question of whether C. Auguste Dupin or Sherlock Holmes was the most important fictional detective, I would deserve it.

But the first part of the evening turned out to be much more enjoyable than I had expected, and the last part ended with a shock I won't soon forget.

Simpson's in the Strand, just a short walk from our hotel, was opened in 1828. From advance research, I knew that it was best known for carving beef at the table and for its role in the history of British chess. We sat in one of the very booths once occupied by the legendary chess great Henry Staunton and his mates.

You're probably ahead of me on the restaurant's Sherlockian connections—Holmes and Watson ate there in two stories, "The Adventure of the Dying Detective" and "The Adventure of the Illustrious Client." Simpson's website even lists Sherlock Holmes among its famous patrons, along with Charles Dickens, Vincent van Gogh, and George Bernard Shaw.

Well, okay, but none of them were at our table that night before the great debate, just Professor Althea Ralston and Sir Stephen Fresch. Neither one was quite what I had expected. Sir Stephen was balding, in his early sixties, with a thick mustache and a not-so-thick Eastern European accent. I wouldn't have pegged him for an innovative captain of industry, but then, what do I know?

Ralston was the big surprise, though. No aging academic, she was just a little older than me—say, around forty—and striking in appearance. She had pure white hair like Andy Warhol, worn ear length, and a strand of white pearls across her slender chest. Her complexion was pale, the opposite of Lynda's. Everything else about her was either black or gray. She wore a long black skirt, a light gray blouse of soft material under a black bolero jacket with sequins, and obsidian earrings. I could imagine her smoking a cigarette through a long, black holder, like a socialite in a *New Yorker* cartoon.

"Althea is the perfect moderator for our little debate," Mac rumbled after we had gone through the introduction ritual. "As a historian, she is perfectly neutral."

"Not exactly," Ralston said, sounding veddy, veddy British. "It's quite true that as between Holmes and Dupin, I could argue both sides as to which was the most important fictional detective, but I have my preferences in the genre."

"She likes the tough guys," Sir Stephen said. "I've read your book, Professor."

My ears perked up. "I haven't had that pleasure," I told Ralston. "Tell me about it."

Lynda rolled her eyes. She never did share my affection for hard-boiled private eyes, and now she had fallen for Sherlock Holmes. We've agreed to disagree about our different literary tastes. I thought I'd been a pretty good sport about what had largely turned into a Sherlockian pilgrimage to London. I didn't even complain about being dragged to Baker Street. So I felt that a little side trip onto the darker side of the street was not asking too much.

"It's called *Murder Without Manners*," Ralston said. I wondered whether she dyed her hair white; Warhol had. "It's a critical history of the detective story, finding elements of the hard-boiled hero in some unexpected quarters. In other words, it's not just about Sam Spade, Philip Marlowe, Amos Walker, and so forth, or the characters of James Hadley Chase and Peter Cheyney on this side of the ocean.

"For example, Rex Stout's Nero Wolfe may be in the mold of the eccentric sleuth like Dupin or Holmes, but Archie Goodwin would have been quite at home with the other tough guys in *Black Mask* magazine. It was Stout's particular genius to successfully combine the two strains and attract the fans of both."

"Mike Hammer is a long way from Baker Street," I pointed out. "I suppose you're not a Holmesian."

"On the contrary!" She pronounced the last word almost as if it only had two syllables. Her gray eyes gleamed. "I'm a member of the Sherlock Holmes Society of London. Holmes has a lot in common with your American private eyes. Like them, he's something of a vigilante, a free agent who often breaks the law in the name of justice. And even though he's a professional, he can't be bought and often works for free."

This was ringing a bell. I'd heard something of the kind a while back in Erin at a talk delivered by my favorite private eye writer, Al Kane. I didn't buy it then, either.

Ralston paused to sip a Bombay Sapphire martini, straight up. Refueled, she ploughed on:

"I think the second half of the last Holmes novel, *The Valley of Fear*, is a ripping good hard-boiled detective story about Birdie Edwards, and I agree with Steven Doyle that it was the first of that sub-genre ever written. Many of the later Holmes stories have a lot of grit, almost like *film noir*. For example . . ."

And so forth. She kind of lost me for a while. It wouldn't be fair to say she was full of herself, but she was certainly full of her subject—and gin. I kind of perked up when she shifted topics and said, "I've enjoyed reading your books about Mac's adventures, Jeff. I must say, you are even handsomer than the photo on the back cover. Have you ever thought of writing your own mystery novel?"

"You wouldn't believe it if I told you," I said. The subject of my multiple unpublished Max Cutter adventures was still a bit of sore spot with me.

At some point, after drinks and before dinner, Kate managed to gracefully turn the conversation toward Sir Stephen. My sister was wearing a peaked cap, perched jauntily over her piles of hair, and the Sherlock Holmes tie she'd bought in Baker Street. "How is it that an Englishman comes to be the premier collector and defender of America's Edgar Allan Poe?" she asked.

He chuckled. Light from a chandelier danced off of his bald pate. "Perhaps the better question is how I came to be an Englishman! The small town in which I was born under a different name is now part of Poland. The opportunities there under the old communist regime when I was a boy were, shall we say, somewhat limited.

"Well, I won't bore you with the details of my illegal and harrowing journey, but I left when I was very young. I intended to make my way to your United States because I have always admired America. I thought England was just a way-station." He smiled. "But I stayed because this country has been very good to me. I made my fortune here." He frowned. "Apparently I have lost a good deal of it here as well. It seems that millions of pounds that I entrusted to Phillimore have been lost, and a lot of my investment gains were never real. I only hope that I am not ruined!" He gulped the scotch in front of him, his face flushed. "That bastard, I wish I had him here!"

I looked at Lynda. Behind her comely oval face, I could see the wheels churning. Perhaps Sir Stephen would consent to an interview about what it felt like to be screwed by a fellow billionaire. My own reaction was somewhat more gut-level. *Maybe that Fresch Air plane we flew in on from Venice will be repossessed. Good thing we're flying home on Delta.*

"Try to keep your mind on Poe, just for tonight," Lynda told Fresch in a transparent attempt to ingratiate herself with a potential interviewee. "You need to be up for the debate. You were explaining how you came to be a collector of Poe."

The dark clouds on the Fresch countenance cleared. "Perhaps it's my admiration for all things American that led to my obsession for Edgar Allan Poe, a true American original. I have read his stories since I was a boy and I have been collecting his books and manuscripts for decades now."

"I am afraid that will not be enough tonight, Sir Stephen," Mac said cheerfully. "No doubt you are a worthy antagonist, but I have the better argument."

"I think not," Sir Stephen said with the assurance of the fabulously wealthy. "I have a silver bullet. By the end of the evening, I assure you, even you will concede I won the debate."

Chapter Twelve
Hot Air vs. Fresch Air

"You should have had the Silver Fox as a history teacher," Lynda said with a strained smile as we took our seats in the auditorium at King's Strand campus.

"????" (That was the look on my face.)

"You were hanging on every word she said."

"Only the first part," I corrected. "When she said 'Sherlock Holmes,' I kind of zoned out until she started talking about my writing."

Lynda looked skeptical.

If I didn't know better, love of my life, I'd think you were just a smidgen jealous. But that never happens to you, does it? Jealousy is my gig!

"What are you smiling about?"

Before I had a chance to explain that I was just reveling anew in the joys of the marital state, Faro came on stage to welcome the assembled multitudes, a hundred people at most, to The Great C. Auguste Dupin–Sherlock Holmes Debate. Standing at a podium, he looked suitably professorial with his long, squared-off Walt Whitman beard.

Curiously, there didn't seem to be many young people in the audience. Where were the students? I figured the gray-hairs (or the white-hair, in the case of Althea Ralston, a.k.a. "the Silver Fox") could have included faculty as well as members of the Binomial Theorists and the Sherlock Holmes Society of London. Faro had introduced us to one of the Theorists when we arrived at the auditorium, a stiff-upper-lip type in his early forties with a blondish mustache presented as Mr. Aiden Kingsley, Member of Parliament. Apparently we were supposed to know his name because he was also a novelist of some repute, but the moniker didn't strike a bell with me.

"Before the first verbal volleys of this stimulating debate are launched, it is my pleasure as a representative of the Binomial Theorists of London to announce the winner of our pastiche-writing contest," Faro began. "A panel of distinguished Sherlockians, led by Professor Sebastian McCabe"—he nodded in Mac's direction—"have given the laurels to a story called 'The Adventure of the Magic Umbrella,' based on the canonical references to the strange disappearance of Mr. James Phillimore. Unfortunately, the author, Mr. Arthur James Phillimore, cannot accept the prize because he has disappeared."

I guess I was too close to the situation to laugh. Most of the others in the auditorium weren't under that handicap, even though they all had to know that Phillimore's exit from the scene just ahead of Scotland Yard was no joke to thousands of his investors.

They were still laughing as Faro ceded the stage to Althea Ralston and the two combatants. Faro joined Kate, Lynda, and me in one of the front rows. Ralston went through the very simple rules of the debate, which specified that cheering and booing were not only permitted but were encouraged. Maybe this was to make Mr. Aiden Kingsley, M.P., feel at home.

Luck of the draw had Sir Stephen Fresch speak first. I took notes throughout the debate so I could churn out a press release and an article for our alumni magazine. I even tweeted. But I'm not going to give you all of it, just the highlights on both sides.

"The detective story was already well established by the time the first Sherlock Holmes novel appeared in 1887," Sir Stephen began. "Edgar Allan Poe had invented it in the

1840s. Poe wrote only short stories, but Charles Dickens, Wilkie Collins, Émile Gaboriau, and Anna Katherine Green expanded the genre to novel form in England, France and the United States, respectively. Sherlock Holmes even commented to Dr. Watson on his fictional predecessors during the early days of their friendship, calling Gaboriau's Lecoq 'a miserable bungler' and Poe's amateur sleuth Auguste Dupin 'a very inferior fellow' who was 'by no means such a phenomenon as Poe appeared to imagine.'

"However, when an admirer of Poe attacked Conan Doyle in verse in 1912 for this dismissal of the American writer, Conan Doyle separated himself from his character's attitudes in a poetic response called 'To Undiscerning Critic.' He ended his verse with these often-quoted words:

"'He, the created, would scoff and would sneer,
Where I, the creator, would bow and revere.
So please grip this fact with your cerebral tentacle:
The doll and its maker are never identical.'"

That drew the biggest laugh of the night, even though it was so familiar to some that I noticed a few audience members reciting it silently along with Sir Stephen.

"Conan Doyle was, in fact, a great admirer of Poe. When hearing that William Gillette was going to be touring in Baltimore, he asked this actor so famous for bringing Sherlock Holmes to life on the stage to place a wreath on Poe's tomb for him. And in his memoirs, Conan Doyle wrote: 'If every man who receives a cheque for a story which owes its inspiration to Poe were to pay a tithe to a monument for the master, he would have a pyramid as big as that of Cheops. He is not only the root, but one of the flowers on his own stem.'

"Nor was Conan Doyle wrong, or even exaggerating. In the course of his three Dupin tales plus 'The Gold Bug,' Poe established such familiar conventions as the eccentric amateur detective, the admiring friend, the bumbling police, the least likely suspect solution, the locked room mystery, the hidden-in-plain-sight gambit, and the cipher that must be solved."

Then Sir Stephen went on to draw what he thought were parallels between the three Dupin stories and Sherlock Holmes stories fifty years later, which I thought was stretching it a bit.

"There's no denying that Sherlock Holmes is the most famous detective in the world," he said as he reached his conclusion. "His deerstalker hat and magnifying glass mean detective all over the globe. Everybody has heard of Sherlock Holmes and almost nobody has heard of C. Auguste Dupin. But the question was not which character is best known, but which was more influential and therefore most important. And the answer to that question, ladies and gentlemen, can only be Chevalier Dupin!"

Sir Stephen sat down to a smattering of polite applause, this being a Holmes-friendly crowd. But I gave him full marks for cleverness in the way he framed the debate at the end so that popularity was taken off the table as part of the argument. U.S. presidential candidates could learn from that. I'm almost certain that Mac was forced to cut from his opening statement a boatload of statistics on books sold, movies made, sets tuned to the BBC's *Sherlock*, and groups like the Baker Street Irregulars and the Sherlock Holmes Society of London. Instead, he began with:

"Without Dupin, there never would have been a Sherlock Holmes. But without Sherlock Holmes, the detective story might never have become the almost universally appreciated genre that it is today. Conan Doyle took Poe's formula, improved upon it by almost always playing fair with the reader, and popularized it to a degree that Poe could scarcely have imagined. He achieved an enviable commercial and critical success, which inevitably inspired imitators and successors in the field.

"And how did he do that?"

Mac proceeded to answer his own question, but I missed it. I heard a little "ping" noise and Faro, sitting next to me on the left, pulled out his phone and looked at the screen. After a minute he started typing furiously with both thumbs like a digital native.

"Hot news," I whispered to Lynda on my right.

"The latest on the Miley Cyrus nuptials, no doubt," she responded archly.

But I wasn't so sure. I tore my attention back to the debate, but I still thought something big might be happening.

There were more comments and rebuttals until each debater had the opportunity to make a final statement. Sir Stephen rose to the occasion. After a summary of his previous arguments, he concluded by saying:

"If all that means nothing to you, then consider this, ladies and gentlemen: Sherlock Holmes cannot be the most important fictional character because, according to his most ardent fans, he is not *fictional!*"

With that, he abruptly sat down as the audience exploded in applause, the loudest coming from the Sherlockians.

If Mac had had a cigar in his mouth at that moment, he would have swallowed it. He stared at Sir Stephen, then at the audience, and then at Althea Ralston.

"Madame Moderator," he intoned solemnly, "in the face of truth I have no rebuttal. I concede the debate."

The response from the crowd was about half and half between laughter and applause. I was one of the clappers, glad that it was over.

As soon as the commotion died down a bit, I turned to Faro. "Something's up. What is it?"

He didn't bother to deny it or stall. "It's Phillimore. Scotland Yard found him at the Langham Hotel. He apparently shot himself to death."

Excerpt from the Professor's Journal
June 10, 2012

Phillimore was a greater fool than I imagined. His suspicion of me was even more obvious at the end. He was a bundle of nerves when I came to his room at the Langham. And yet he did nothing to protect himself from me. Killing him was just no challenge at all. Now it's up to McCabe to make this interesting. I still have hopes.

Chapter Thirteen
"It Simply Does Not Make Sense"

We didn't get much sleep that night. After the auditorium cleared out, Lynda interviewed Sir Stephen and then wrote a story for the Grier wire. She got him to hold forth not only on his feelings about being out millions of pounds in a Ponzi scheme, but his reaction to the news that Phillimore had killed himself ("I'm speechless," followed by a paragraph full of such phrases as "feel so betrayed," "coward's way out," and "complicates the situation").

Then I had to endure Mac's lecture on the important history of the Langham Hotel. Arthur Conan Doyle and Oscar Wilde had dined with an American magazine publisher there in 1889. The result had been Conan Doyle's *The Sign of Four* and Wilde's *The Picture of Dorian Gray*. Several characters from the Canon had stayed there, most notably the King of Bohemia, but apparently they had all had better experiences than Phillimore.

Faro's column was once again occupying page one of *The Daily Eye* the next morning with a piece comparing Phillimore's exit to that of Robert Maxwell, a British publishing baron who apparently fell off his yacht in the Canary Islands and drowned in 1991. After he died it turned out that he'd stolen money from his companies' pension funds to keep the empire afloat. His sons had to declare bankruptcy.

"That's a pretty flimsy analogy," Lynda complained. "I hate it when reporters do that."

Mac, sitting at breakfast with us in our hotel restaurant, had a different concern. "Why the devil would Phillimore go to all that trouble to disappear in such a dramatic fashion and then kill himself? It simply does not make sense."

"Don't suicides often do things that don't make sense?" Kate said. "Hedda Bortz back in Erin set out her cereal bowl at the breakfast table right before she took an overdose of sleeping pills on the day that guy she dated for seventeen years married her sister Minnie."

"Hedda Bortz was *non compos mentis* to begin with," Mac grumbled, "as proven by the fact that she dated Ralph Hollis for seventeen years. Minnie divorced him after six months."

Fascinating as this discussion might have been (to somebody), I was listening with only half an ear as I read through the sidebar on Faro's column. The piece was obviously written earlier and originally intended to be Faro's daily contribution to world knowledge before it was upstaged by Phillimore's death. It listed the movie actors, reality-TV stars, athletes, politicians, wealthy entrepreneurs and executives, and even charitable institutions who had been Phillimore clients. It was like Bernie Madoff with a British accent, although there were plenty of fish from the American side of the ocean caught in the net as well.

When I had a chance to get a word in edgewise, I called my tablemates' attention to the sidebar. "It's a who's who of big money people," I said. "At least, they used to have big money."

"I wonder where Faro got all those names," Lynda said.

"Most likely from his sources at Scotland Yard, one of whom almost certainly is a fellow Binomial Theorist," Mac said, clearly referring to Assistant Commissioner Madigan, Faro's pal at the Brigadiers Club. He paused as if struck by a thought. "Now that is curious."

I'll bite. "What?"

"I am not privy to the entire membership list of that exclusive group, but so far as I know not one member of the Binomial Theorists appears on that list of Phillimore victims."

Lynda shrugged, expressing my sentiments exactly. "So he didn't cheat his friends," she said. "What's strange about that?"

"Everything! It is almost a cliché that when a con man is exposed many of the victims will say in interviews that they had been friends for years. I believe you would find that was true in the Madoff case. Of course, I could be wrong." *You don't really believe that.* "Perhaps some of the victims are members of the Binomial Theorists whose names have never come to my attention. It is a rather quiet group, as well as an elite one. Its members do not publish books and papers or—"

"Or engage in some of the public frivolities that consume the more extroverted Holmes groups." The portly figure of Welles Faro had appeared in our midst, standing over Mac's shoulder. Lynda squeezed my hand. His voice must have reached her ears with all the charm of a fingernail scratched on a chalk board. He was not her favorite fellow.

"We aren't quite like Mycroft Holmes's Diogenes Club, whose members were absolutely forbidden to speak to each other on pain of expulsion," Faro continued, "but we have kept a rather low profile. Even sponsoring the pastiche contest was a bit of a step out for us."

"I was just observing that your members seemed to have been surprisingly fortunate at avoiding Phillimore Investments," Mac said.

Faro shrugged. "None of our names is on the list, that's true enough. Our purpose as a club is social, not business."

"How did you get that list?" Lynda asked. Maybe she hoped to surprise the answer out of Faro by the bluntness of her question.

"Ah, that would be telling, and I never reveal my sources." I'm sure Faro considered his tone humorous. I'm equally sure that Lynda, in the tradition of a former British monarch, Was Not Amused. "In fact, I'm just on my way to catch up on a few sources now. Thought I'd drop around first and see how you survived the night."

Just great. Who needs sleep?

"So what's today's scoop for the all-seeing *Daily Eye?*" Lynda asked, apparently trying to sound downright perky. The three cups of caffeine-laced coffee that she'd consumed before and during breakfast probably helped.

Faro chuckled. "I get paid very well to save that kind of information for my readers. But I can tell you—"

He didn't, though, because just then Lynda's cell phone rang. It's a very boring ringtone that came with the phone. She pulled the phone out of her purse, looked at the number calling, and stood up. "Excuse me," she said on her way out of the room.

"Yes, Welles," Mac prompted.

Faro had been watching Lynda, a little closely for my comfort, but he turned back to Mac. "I'm sure all the media will have this, but Scotland Yard has assigned Inspector Neville Heath to look into Phillimore's death, reporting to Andy Madigan."

Mac raised an eyebrow. Kate said, "You mean they suspect it was something other than a suicide?"

"Of course not, my dear! It's just that when a swindler on a massive scale disappears and then turns up dead, one has to be sure. Heath's a good man, but he has one weakness: I happen to know that he harbors a secret ambition to be a mystery writer. And one of his favorite sleuths is your Damon Devlin, Professor McCabe."

"I shall endeavor not to hold that against him," Mac said with a painful attempt to not seem pleased by that last bit of intel.

"Well, the day is getting on," Faro said. *Wow, yeah, it'll be noon in just four hours!* "I'd best be going."

Nobody tried to stop him.

He'd barely left when Lynda returned with an excited expression on her face. "That was Assistant Commissioner Madigan. He agreed to my request for an interview. And here's the super-weird part: He asked me to bring along my husband and my brother-in-law."

Chapter Fourteen
Scotland Yard

Max Cutter, the hard-boiled Philadelphia private eye who is the hero of all seven of my unpublished mystery novels, would probably never be allowed inside New Scotland Yard. That's just one of the differences between us.

"You ought to go with us," I told Kate. "They don't do tours of the Yard. It would be something different."

"Not different enough for me," Kate said. "I live with a mystery writer. I get enough of Scotland Yard from him. Besides, I want to visit the National Portrait Gallery and there's no sense in dragging the rest of you along."

You don't have to be a tea-swilling fan of Inspector Whosis on PBS to feel at least a little thrill at hearing the two words "Scotland Yard." The name carries a romantic resonance that the initials FBI lack. The concrete barriers around the building and the armed guards patrolling it did nothing to disabuse me of the notion that this was a no-nonsense outfit. So, of course, inside we had to show our IDs, sign our names, march through a metal detector, and so forth. After about fifteen minutes of that rigmarole, we finally got hustled into the Assistant Commissioner's office.

When I say the Assistant Commissioner, I don't mean *the* Assistant Commissioner. There are four of them. I don't know how their responsibilities are divided, but apparently AC Andrew Madigan was in charge of mopping up swindles against rich and important people. This merited an office four times the size of mine, though probably not humongous by corporate standards.

I'd seen Madigan from a distance at the Brigadiers Club when he'd been leaving Faro. Closer up, I still thought his high forehead and prominent, patrician nose were worth a "Sir" in front of his name, and I figured he'd get one eventually.

"Welcome to New Scotland Yard," he said, extending his hand to each of us in turn. "Thanks for coming in. You men may wonder why I asked for you to join Ms. Teal. I'll get to that presently. But first, I believe Ms. Teal has some questions for me."

"That I do. Thanks for taking the time to see me, Assistant Commissioner." Lynda flipped out her notebook and a small recording device. "Do you mind if I record this? Good. I want to be accurate. Let's start with Phillimore. He fooled a lot of people. The list of his victims reads like a *Who's Who* of entertainment, the arts, business, and politics on both sides of the Atlantic. I even noticed the name of Moon Kelso, lead drummer for Orange Zebra." That's one of Lynda's favorite groups. "Phillimore must have been special. What can you tell me about him that I don't know from the other media?"

It was an excellent question. Madigan smiled at the way she phrased it.

"I suppose he was a bit of a con man from the get-go. He liked to give the impression that he was the son of some minor royal, born on the wrong side of the blanket. In point of fact, his father drove a lorry." *That's "truck" in American.* "He was a bright lad, good enough to get a scholarship to Winchester College, one of our most prestigious public schools—what you would call a private school in America." *Of course, private is public in England.*

"He took a first in finance at Oxford and landed a job at Lloyd's Bank. He built a reputation for being good at investments, which he parlayed into starting his own firm. At this stage of the investigation, we believe that Phillimore Investments was legitimate in the beginning. It appears that during the last recession he didn't want his clients to know that the value of their holdings had diminished greatly. In order to maintain his reputation as an investment sage, he falsified their returns. When any of them cashed out, he took the money from new clients."

"A classic Ponzi scheme," Lynda noted, thanks to my tutorial on Saturday. "I understand that you were a friend of Phillimore."

Madigan nodded. "You could say that, applying the term rather loosely. We didn't dine at each others' houses, but we saw each other with some frequency because we shared a certain interest. When I got wind of the investigation, I immediately alerted the Commissioner of my potential conflict of interests. He decided that, having disclosed the relationship, there was no reason that I should remove myself from supervision of the case."

"How did the investigation begin?" Lynda asked. "Who blew the whistle?"

"That I am not at liberty to say."

"Was it a client or an employee?" my favorite journalist pressed.

"Again, that is something I'm afraid I can't discuss while the investigation is ongoing."

"So Phillimore's death changes nothing?"

"Oh, I wouldn't say that. It may make our task more difficult in some ways as we try to untangle all of this."

"How close were you to an arrest?"

"I wouldn't want to speculate on that, but I've already indicated that we have not completed the investigation."

The interview went on for another fifteen minutes or so. Mac and I kept our peace while Lynda asked questions about how long the investigation might take (probably weeks rather than months), the size of the fraud (certainly billions, but not even estimated yet), the possibility that others in Phillimore's company were involved ("almost certainly"), etc.

"Is there any question I haven't asked yet that I should have?" Lynda said at the end.

"I can't think of any," Madigan said. "But I would like to make this statement. If anyone has information that would be helpful in our inquiries, we would be most eager to have your cooperation even if you were a party to this crime." *Translation: Let's make a deal.*

Madigan stood up. "Now I would like you to meet the investigating officer in Phillimore's death. He is eager to talk to you gentlemen because you were on the scene when Phillimore disappeared. He's already talked to Mr. Faro."

"Will this conversation be on the record for me?" Lynda asked.

"That's up to Inspector Heath, Ms. Teal."

Inspector Neville Heath had a smaller office than Madigan and a heartier manner. He was taller than me, with big ears and black hair combed back, wearing a double-breasted gray pinstriped suit like Humphrey Bogart in *The Maltese Falcon.* I figured he was in his late forties. He reminded me of somebody, but I couldn't figure out whom.

Heath approached Mac with an outstretched hand. "Sebastian McCabe." He said it the way Lynda once pronounced the name of a legendary master distiller she met during a bourbon-tasting that she coerced me into. "I have all of your books." *They make good doorstops, don't they?*

"Very kind of you to say so," Mac responded.

The love fest went on for a while before Heath acknowledged Lynda and me and got down to business. "I've taken a statement from Mr. Welles Faro about the events leading up to Mr. Phillimore's disappearance, but I thought it might be helpful to get your perspective as well."

My brother-in-law, the raconteur, started the story from when we arrived in front of Headley Hall. The inspector interrupted frequently with questions, even asking what Phillimore's jacket looked like. "It was a classic blue blazer with brass buttons," Mac said. Lynda scribbled in her notebook. Heck, I could have told her that.

"Taking notes, Ms. Teal?" Heath said.

"Do you mind?"

"Not yet. I'll let you know when we're off the record." He turned back to Mac. "You're sure that he had this Conan Doyle notebook he talked about?"

"Sure?" Mac shook his head. "Strictly speaking, no. All I can assert from my own observation is that he patted his breast pocket and said that he had it. I never actually saw it. Why?"

"Because it wasn't on his body, even though he was apparently wearing the same blue blazer."

"Is that important?" Mac asked.

"I doubt it. But it's an anomaly. I always pay attention to anomalies. Well, he probably left it in the house somewhere. I'm sure it will turn up. Go on, Mr. McCabe."

As Mac continued the story, Heath asked a lot of questions about his thought processes and research leading up to the discovery of the priest hole.

"Incredible," he said. "Just like one of your books."

Mac begged to differ. "My books are not incredible, Inspector. At least, I hope not. Fiction must be plausible, even when it is impossible."

Heath chuckled. "I'll keep that in mind, should I ever commit a mystery novel. Now tell me, and you, too, Mr. Cody, what sort of mood would you say that Mr. Phillimore was in when you last saw him?"

"Downright ebullient," I said. I love that word because it sounds like what it means.

"Well, said, Jefferson!" Mac praised. "That is just the descriptive adjective I would choose. He was also animated and friendly."

"No signs of depression then?"

"Not at all," I said.

"Well, that's not unusual with suicides."

"Do you have any idea why he killed himself?" Lynda asked. "Presumably he didn't know that he was being investigated, so that wasn't it."

"Ah, but apparently he *did* know, somehow," Heath said. "At least, that's the way I read the suicide note."

Lynda's gold-flecked brown eyes gleamed as she jumped on that. "Faro's story didn't say anything about a suicide note!"

"We just found out this morning. Phillimore sent a final text message to his wife—one of my favorite actresses, by the way. Ms. O'Toole didn't recognize it as such at the time because the language was rather indirect."

Spread out on Heath's desk were the personal effects that Phillimore had taken with him to the Langham. *The Penguin Complete Sherlock Holmes*, a fat paperback with the detective's image on the front, was the give-away on that. Heath picked up a smartphone. "Here. See for yourself."

Phillimore had written:

It's all coming apart. I cannot bear the stain on my honor. This was the only way out. Please forgive me.

His wife responded.

U coward. Come back here and face the music. But don't contact me again. Call my lawyer. I hate u!

There was no response.

"What lovebirds," I muttered.

"This is all wrong," Mac said. "Phillimore did not write this."

"What do you mean? How do you figure that?" Lynda asked before Heath or I could.

"No Englishman would spell 'honor' that way. He would use the British spelling of h-o-n-o-u-r. This message must have been written by an American, or someone who speaks American English."

For a few seconds it was like time stopped. Nobody moved or said anything. Finally, Heath broke the silence. "Well, let's not get carried away and make a murder mystery out of it. Perhaps Phillimore was just in a hurry or a poor speller."

"Tell me about the gun," Mac said.

"It was a Colt .32."

"Yes, I read that. That's a fairly common gun in America." Mac himself owns one. I'm always afraid he's going to shoot himself with it on the rare occasions when he sticks it into his belt. "Did it belong to Phillimore?"

"His wife didn't know. There wouldn't be a record of it. Guns bigger than .22 are illegal here in the UK, except for Northern Ireland."

"May I look at the crime scene photos?"

"Right here." Heath shoved them across the desk at Mac.

As Mac studied the photos, I looked over his shoulder. Phillimore's head was a bloody mess, his body flopped to one side in a chair.

"So he shot himself on the right side of his head with the gun in his right hand while he was sitting in the chair next to the table. After firing, he dropped the gun and slumped over." He looked up. "I suppose Phillimore was right-handed?"

"Oh, yes, sir. We checked that. Bit of a cliché, isn't it—the suicide with the gun in the wrong hand? You wouldn't put that in a story, would you?"

"I wouldn't dare," Mac mumbled, still looking at the photos. "Here's something interesting." He pointed at one of the photos. "Look at that drinking glass under the table."

"What about it?" Heath said.

"It's not far from Phillimore's right hand. Doesn't it look as if it fell out of it? He couldn't have had the glass in that hand if he also had a gun in it."

"The report noted the stain and the odor of scotch on the carpet," Heath said. "Perhaps he'd been drinking heavily, dropped the glass, and didn't think it was worth cleaning up before he picked up the gun to end it all."

"That is possible," Mac conceded. "However, when coupled with the obviously bogus suicide message, I find it implausible."

"So how do you walk up to somebody in his own hotel room and shoot him?" Lynda asked.

"I would suggest that with Phillimore 'the worse for drink,' as they say, he was in no condition to appreciate the threat coming or to resist."

"A killer could scarcely count on being able to get him drunk," Heath protested.

"Certainly not," Mac agreed. "The murder could have been unpremeditated, a crime of opportunity carried out precisely *because* Phillimore was so vulnerable. I suspect premeditation, however. You might want to have a toxicology report run, Inspector, to see if there were any drugs in his body at the time of his death. That would accelerate the effects of the alcohol."

"I'd like to back up a little," Lynda said. "What do you think about this murder idea, Inspector?"

"Before I answer that, we'd better go off the record. Anything I say now will be speculation and I don't want to be accused of sensationalism."

Lynda rolled her eyes. "Oh, no, we'll leave the sensationalism to Faro. All right, I agree to keep it under my hat, which I'm not wearing, until you're ready to say something official. But I want to be the first to get the official word."

"Right, then. Publicly, this remains a suicide investigation. Privately, Mr. McCabe has made a rather convincing case and I am no longer certain that Mr. Phillimore ended his own life. I'm far from convinced, but this could indeed be a matter of murder."

"Well, you've got about a thousand suspects," I burst out. "Or however many people he defrauded."

"First the victim would have to know that he or she was a victim before the Ponzi scheme story broke." Mac stroked his beard. "He or she could have come to that knowledge in any number of ways. The problem with the victim-as-killer theory is that, satisfying though homicide might be, it does nothing of itself to fill the pocketbook. A lawsuit might have been a more suitable response. Of course, the killer could also sue the estate as well as taking the more drastic action. No doubt many victims will.

"What strikes me most about our theoretical killer is that he or she had to know that Phillimore was hiding out at the Langham. Who would know that?"

"That's easy—whoever helped him stage his disappearance from Headley Hall," Lynda said.

"Precisely," Mac agreed.

"We know somebody must have helped him," I said. "And you're saying that person also killed him?"

"Who better to know where he disappeared to?" Mac said. "Incidentally, why did Phillimore disappear?"

"Because he knew the Yard was on to him." Heath's eyes got bigger—not as big as his ears, but bigger. "I see what you're getting at. A leak at the Yard would be a very serious matter. We're quite sensitive about that sort of thing just now."

Scotland Yard was still reeling from the revelation that the Metropolitan Police had bungled the investigation of phone hacking by the now-defunct *News of the World*, and perhaps even covered up the crimes.

"Whether that means murder or not," Lynda said, "it's definitely a story. And I can write it without using anything that's off the record."

Chapter Fifteen
The Son Also Rises

What Lynda had in mind was obvious: A story raising questions about how Phillimore knew his empire of fraud was "coming apart," as the putative suicide message put it. A few new facts, a few quotes, and a lot of background would do it. After picking up some innocuous on-the-record comments from Heath to throw in, she could barely wait to get out of his office and start writing.

Just outside the building, though, we heard, "Mr. McCabe!"

Mac turned around.

A guy about my age, dressed in a tailored three-button black suit was walking our way. In a cartoon or a slapstick comedy, his appearance would have called for me to do a double take. He looked like a younger version of the late Arthur James Phillimore to a startling degree, but with dark hair instead of gray. He even had the dimple, although he had skipped the pencil mustache.

"Yes, I'm McCabe."

"I thought I recognized you. Saw you on the telly once. My name is Roger Phillimore. I understand from *The Daily Eye* that you're caught up in this mess with my father."

What's a GQ dude like you doing reading that rag?

Mac raised an eyebrow. "Caught up? Yes, that seems to be all too true. You have my sympathy, Mr. Phillimore."

"Sympathy?" He seemed taken aback. "Save it for somebody who needs it. If my father wasn't dead, I'd be tempted to kill him myself."

You wouldn't say that if you knew he'd been murdered. Or would you? Those British mystery writers like Agatha Christie always love the old double bluff—the murderer doing just what everybody figurers the murderer wouldn't do.

Lynda pulled out her notebook and started scribbling.

"I imagine that a lot of your father's investors feel that way, Mr. Phillimore," Mac said. "Oh, meet my brother-in-law and his wife."

Hurried handshakes ensued.

"I didn't have a penny invested with my father, but I'm one of his biggest victims," Roger Phillimore said. "He's ruined the Phillimore name, and in my business reputation is everything."

"Your business?" Lynda prodded.

He seemed to really notice her for the first time. *Maybe he's not into tall, stacked, pretty women with curly hair the color of dark honey. It takes all kinds.*

"I'm the managing partner of a private equity firm, RJP Capital," he said. "We acquire troubled companies, usually with a leveraged buyout, introduce efficiencies to make them successful, and then either sell them or take them public."

I can see where you might want to change your last name before you try to put your next deal together.

"Were you coming to Scotland Yard or did you just happen to be in the neighborhood?" Mac asked dryly.

"I want to talk to whomever is investigating my father's so-called suicide. I think they should take a close look at my stepmother. And if they don't, then maybe you should since you're reckoned to be quite the amateur sleuth."

"You suspect murder?" Lynda asked, in a skeptical tone that suggested the idea was a novelty, the furthest thing from anybody else's mind.

"My father viewed obstacles that stopped others in their tracks as nothing more than annoyances to be overcome. Why would a man like that kill himself? He always believed he would win in the end."

Well, the end has come and he's not looking like a winner right now. I saw the pictures.

"How do you arrive at the conclusion that Heather O'Toole is responsible for what you believe was your father's murder?" Mac asked.

"It adds up. She's his sole heir and they haven't been getting along, from what I hear." He shook his head in an attempt to look doleful. "I never thought that marriage was for the long haul—Heather's younger than I am."

"But still, murder?" Lynda said. "Isn't that a bit extreme?"

"I know that woman. I wouldn't put anything past her."

"What makes you so sure she's your father's only heir?" I asked. That kind of thing isn't usually public knowledge, unless Phillimore chose to bandy it about.

Phillimore tried to get taller. "I disinherited myself when he divorced my mother two years ago. I told him I didn't want anything to do with his money. I have enough of my own. I'm sure he was only too happy to honor my wishes. Since he had no favorite charities except himself, I presume the money went to her."

"But there's probably nothing for her to inherit but what you yourself called a mess," Lynda pointed out. "This could drag through the courts for years as the investors try to salvage something, possibly even going after personal assets outside the company."

"I'm sure Heather didn't bother her pretty little head about my father's business. She didn't know it was all a house of cards just waiting for a good wind to blow it over."

Nice metaphor. I made a mental note of it.

"Heather O'Toole has a substantial income stream of her own," Mac pointed out. "Actresses of Bond girl stature do not get paid minimum wage. And surely there was a prenuptial agreement that would settle a sum of money on her if they divorced."

"Right." I love the way the British say that. "But prenup or no, working through that kind of thing takes an army of lawyers and lots of time. Heather isn't a patient woman."

"What about your mother, the first Mrs. Phillimore?" Lynda said. "If somebody killed your father, it seems to me she'd have as good a motive as anybody— woman scorned and all that."

Phillimore shook his head. "No, no, no. You don't know my mother. I would swear that she was totally faithful to my father for thirty-six years, but she took a sizeable settlement from him at the divorce and hasn't looked back. She's not the wife you need to look into."

"I do not suppose you have anything to offer Scotland Yard—or us—in the way of proof," Mac said, "or you would have mentioned it."

"Proof is your department. You're the detectives and I wish you good luck with it." He turned around, heading toward the building from which we'd come, but then faced us again. "I do have one suggestion: Trout."

"The butler?" I said.

Phillimore smirked. "Butler my arse! If he's a butler I'm the Queen's gardener. Did you ever see a butler with biceps like that? I think you'll find that the service he's been rendering my step-mother is of quite a different nature."

Chapter Sixteen
Bodybuilding

"Whew, there goes a man with an axe to grind," I said as Roger Phillimore headed back to the glass and steel building we'd just left. "We already knew that Trout's not *just* a butler. Heather said he's also her personal trainer and bodyguard."

"Indeed," Mac said. "However, sometimes axe grinders have a valid point. If there is a romantic relationship between Ms. O'Toole and this man Trout, it would certainly be an added incentive to want her husband out of the picture."

"And she's an American!" Lynda almost shouted it. "According to your theory, Mac, the killer must be an American, or somebody who spells like one. That would have been a very clever ploy for the killer to text herself a fake suicide note on Phillimore's phone."

What would Heather O'Toole look like in a prison uniform? Still great! I was conjuring up the image when Lynda added, "Next stop, Headley Hall?"

That was easier said than done. It took us a train and a cab to get there, with the cabbie muttering all the while about some of the major roads already being changed to one-way for the Olympics later in the summer. The rain was no help. That June turned out to be the wettest month in London since the dawn of weather records, and we kept getting caught in it.

Mac had decided not to phone ahead. "If forewarned is forearmed, as the cliché has it, I would prefer that Ms. O'Toole not be forearmed."

A gaggle (herd? flock? pack?) of a half-dozen or so paparazzi, apparently having gotten the word that HO'T was in residence, were camped outside Headley Hall when we finally got there. They stirred en masse and ran our way when they saw us coming. But they relaxed and lowered their cameras when they realized we weren't a bunch of Hollywood stars come to call on the Widow Phillimore. One astute fellow in blue jeans and long hair did give Lynda a second look just to be sure. Who can blame him? Anyway, we sailed past the paparazzi with a jaunty wave.

When Trout opened the door, I immediately thought that maybe Mac was on to something—and the younger Phillimore, too. Trout wasn't dressed like any butler I'd ever seen. He was wearing blue gym shorts and a white sleeveless T-shirt showing off muscles that would give Rod Chance a run for his money. That reminded me that we'd seen Chance, HO'T's first husband, coming out of this house. If we were looking for a romantic relationship, maybe we didn't have to look at the hired help. Then again, Trout didn't exactly look like hired help today.

He regarded us with puzzlement, as if something in his cupboard was out of place.

"Good afternoon, Trout!" Mac said. *Jolly good to see you again, old bean.* "You will not be saying 'you're expected' this time, because we are not. I was hoping that Ms. O'Toole was home and willing to spare us a few moments."

"I'll see, sir. One moment."

Instead of inviting us in, this time he let us stand outside in the drizzle. The temperature was about sixty degrees. Lynda nuzzled up against me under our umbrella. I've had worse waits.

After ten minutes or so, Trout opened the door again. "Ms. O'Toole will see you now." His handsome face, impassive as ever, gave no clue as to whether he approved or not. "Follow me, please."

I don't know what the room to which Trout took us had been built for originally—game room? servants' dining hall?—but now it was outfitted as a gym. When I say "outfitted," I mean that it had all the bells and whistles of Nouveau Shape, where Lynda and I work out back home, and then some.

Heather O'Toole, clad in denim cut-offs and a gray and red Manchester United T-shirt, was running hard on a treadmill. Her black hair was gathered into a ponytail sticking out the back of a white Nike cap and bouncing along behind her. Behind the big lenses and dark frames of the glasses she was wearing, her eyes were their presumably natural brown, not violet. She was glistening with sweat, which detracted not one bit from her wholesome attractiveness. When she saw us, she slowed down to a stop.

"Now what?" she asked. She was either bemused or irritated by our return, but I couldn't decide which. She was an actress, after all. I was determined to keep that in mind.

"First of all, we would like to express our genuine sympathy at the death of your husband," Mac said. "As you know, Jefferson and I met him only once. Even in that short encounter his *joie de vivre* was quite apparent."

Roger Phillimore had rejected Mac's offer of sympathy, but not his young stepmother.

"Thanks." She grabbed a towel and started wiping off the sweat. "You can go now, Bernie."

"Yes, ma'am."

Trout faded away.

"It's been quite a shock, all of this," Heather said. "First, the man disappears. Then, I find out that he was some kind of master swindler. Before I can even process that, he kills himself." She sat down on a weight-lifting bench. "I'm trying to work out the tension. Besides, I'm due back on location in Barbados in three days and I'd better be in shape for the bikini scenes."

Absolutely!

"I think you'll be all right," Lynda said dryly. If she felt overdressed in a white crepe dress under her khaki raincoat while the Hollywood beauty in front of her was wearing gym wear, she gave no hint of it. *Au contraire*, as Mac might say, she seemed quite pleased with herself as she pulled a reporter's notebook out of her purse.

Mac, meanwhile, nodded sympathetically . . . before giving Heather O'Toole a verbal kick in the head. "When last we spoke, your references to your husband were quite negative. You even said if he were on an island somewhere you'd kill him."

"Yeah, I know. I almost feel bad about that. I was really pissed at him. All the investors must be, but I had a lot more invested than anybody else. He was my husband, for crap's sake." Maybe she realized what that sounded like, given that his body was barely cold, because she added: "But I sure as hell didn't want him to kill himself. I never imagined that he would."

"Perhaps he did not."

"What?" Her surprise seemed genuine.

"We have just left New Scotland Yard. Inspector Neville Heath is conducting what he expected to be a routine investigation into your husband's apparent suicide. However, there are several inconsistencies surrounding Mr. Phillimore's death that could point in another direction."

"That's hard to believe," Heather said. "I mean, I've never known anybody who was murdered."

"I did not say murder," Mac pointed out. "Why would you assume that the alternative to suicide is murder and not accident?"

Heather stood up. "People don't shoot themselves in the head by accident unless they're playing Russian roulette. I don't know whether James owned a gun, but if he did, I can't see him playing with it. That's not the kind of risk he took. When he gambled, he did it for big stakes with the odds on his side. And he only gambled in business."

"He must have been interesting to live with," Lynda said.

"You have no idea. He was dynamic, exciting." Her eyes glistened. *Of course, actresses know how to do that.* "If you think I married an old man, you're way wrong. I'm still mad at the bastard for what he did, but when I get over that I'm going to be damned sorry that he's gone. We actually had a pretty good thing going. Don't believe anything you might see on *Access Hollywood*."

"Of course not," Mac assured her. "A woman of your, er, stature is inevitably a gossip magnet. For example, someone suggested to us that you might be romantically involved with Mr. Trout."

She laughed, the kind of laugh that in a movie is sometimes followed by a hearty slap. But she kept her hands to herself. "Bernie? That's rich! I'm not his type."

Mac raised an eyebrow.

"I mean, I'm a woman." *You could say that.* "Bernie plays for the other team. He has no sexual interest in women. You've been talking to that sniveling Roger Phillimore, haven't you? I knew it! I can see it in your faces. That twerp! He's just jealous that his father took me away from him."

Lynda fumbled her notebook, almost dropping it. "You mean you dated Roger before you married his father?"

"Yeah, for a few months. It wasn't that serious. At least *I* wasn't. I met him when his company bought the studio that made one of my early movies. It was one of those leveraged buyout things. He is handsome, I have to

admit that, but dull as dishwater. Nothing like James. When Roger introduced me to his father there were sparks between us right away. Things just happened. I traded up."
Wow, family dinners must have been a little tense after that.

"Nice," Lynda muttered.

"Roger's been spreading gossip about me ever since," Heather said. "He's a sore loser, for starters. Plus, he wanted his father's money, and he thought I was going to wind up with it. Hell, now I don't even know if anything will be left after the smoke clears. I'm expecting massive lawsuits from James's investors over that Ponzi stuff."

"Undoubtedly the situation will be quite complex," Mac said. "As heir to the estate, you—"

"Actually, I don't know whether I am or not," Heather interrupted. "James never told me. Under the prenuptial agreement I signed, I wouldn't get anything if we divorced within five years of our marriage. I've always assumed his will carried a similar provision, but I don't know for sure. And I don't think it matters now that his investors are likely to get whatever assets he had. If anybody benefitted from my husband's death, it wasn't me."

"Suppose you were the detective," I said. "Who would you put under the bright lights?"

"Roger," she said without hesitation. "Or maybe his mother. They must have hated James for leaving her. Killing him might not have gotten them any money, but the psychological satisfaction would be off the charts."

Chapter Seventeen
The Silver Fox

"I need a nap," Lynda said as we approached our hotel.

Be still my beating heart!

"I'm so tired I can't keep my eyes open."

Oh, that kind of nap.

"There will be no nap for you, Jefferson," Mac said. "I am sure you remember that you are going with me to King's College London this afternoon."

"How could I forget?" *It's not like I've had anything else on my mind.*

"Well, have fun," Lynda yawned. "I'm going to write and send my story, then sack out."

Actually, she had already slept on the train, leaving me to ponder in silence what we had so far:

Arthur James Phillimore, Holmesian and swindler extraordinaire, had staged his own dramatic disappearance with the help of an accomplice. Why? Presumably he'd known that Scotland Yard—always portrayed as a bunch of dolts in the Sherlock Holmes stories—was on to his Ponzi scheme.

While his disappearance was causing an international stir, he'd been holed up in the Langham Hotel, a luxury hostelry with a venerable history stretching back to Victorian days and the Holmes Canon. But he didn't enjoy it long because he got a bullet in his head.

Mac was convinced that the suicide note Phillimore seemed to have sent to his wife was a fake produced by a speaker of American English. The dead man's son, Roger Phillimore, pointed the finger at his younger stepmother, who is an American in addition to being gorgeous and famous. Okay, forget the last two adjectives; not relevant. Heather O'Toole thought her stepson, who was also an ex-boyfriend aced out by his father, was a dandy murder suspect, and so was his mother.

I toyed with casting Heather for the role of killer just because it would make a heck of a story. She could have helped him escape, too. No, that's not true. She was in Barbados on Thursday when Phillimore went missing. But she flew back to England right away, so she could have shot him. Wait a minute—she didn't have to. She could have had somebody do her dirty work for her. Trout was handy.

All of this was swirling around my head when we left Lynda at the hotel, where she would write her story and then grab a snooze. I'm sure that data was being processed in the McCabe brain as well, except that he would be two or three steps ahead of me.

King's College London has five campuses. The School of Arts & Humanities, along with several other schools, is housed in the Strand Building, within walking distance of our home-away-from-home. The debate had been held there. It's a nine-story, ultra-modern poured concrete building taking up most of a London city block. The shop peddling school ties, mugs, T-shirts, and all that is housed in an adjacent older structure.

"I am meeting Professor Ralston at two o'clock to discuss our exchange program," Mac said. "Perhaps you would like to spend an hour or so gathering material and then join us."

"Perhaps," I said, meaning yes.

So we figured out where her office was (second floor), and then I went off on my own taking pictures of long hallways, close-ups of a Shakespeare bust, empty classrooms, etc. What I didn't take pictures of was students because there weren't any. The closest I got was a sign in an oak-framed display case saying, "Welcome Study Abroad Students!" I'd expected to find some study abroad students in summer session, like our kids back home.

"Excuse me!" I hailed a fellow carrying a dirty mop that looked a lot like his head of gray hair. "I seem to have misplaced your students. Where are they?"

The maintenance man chuckled. "On 'oliday since May." He pronounced it *My*. "Summer School don't start till July."

No students! How was I going to write a press release, an alumni magazine article, blog posts, and so forth about our students in London without talking to students? Damn Mac! I distinctly remembered that he mentioned me interviewing students. He should have known better.

If I could have gotten my hands around his fat neck at that moment, I'd have wrung it. But that wouldn't have solved my problem. I had to find a way to justify part of this English sojourn as a business trip for St. Benignus. Let's see. The pictures I'd taken would help. And I'd already done a lot of Internet research on King's College. I could talk to Ralston about our students coming here, and then back home I could interview St. Benignus students who were planning to cross the pond to study. Yes, that would work. I'd salvage the situation with a little Yankee ingenuity, no thanks to Mac.

One thought of St. Benignus led to another. Before I knew it, homesickness was nudging me out of my daydreams of fratricide-in-law. I pulled out my phone and sent a text to Popcorn.

JEFF: *What's up? Anything exciting going on?*
POPCORN: *We're just having breakfast at Daniel's.*
JEFF: *"We"?*
POPCORN: *None of your business.*

Hmm. She never does breakfast with her gal pals. Could it be that my widowed administrative assistant had found romance outside those steamy novels by Rosamund DeLacey that she's always reading? Age fifty at her birthday in a few days and determined to stop there, Popcorn is a pleasingly plump little package with dyed blond hair. Standing just under five feet tall, she'd be a great catch for some lucky guy. I'd long suspected that Oscar Hummel wanted to reel her in. But if she didn't want to tell me "what's on," as they say in the UK, that was her business. I certainly wasn't going to pry.

Oscar doesn't have a smartphone, just a dumb one, so I sent him an e-mail: *"So, what's new with you? Been out to breakfast lately? Having wonderful crime here in jolly old England. Wish you were here."*

He'd get back to me eventually, maybe even before I got back home.

Before I knew it, the hour was over and I presented myself at Professor Ralston's second-floor office to rendezvous with Mac.

Seeing Althea Ralston in her natural habitat, an office crammed with books, I had to wonder if she always dressed in black and shades of gray—she must have fifty of them!—to play off of her short white hair. This time she was wearing black teardrop earrings and a sleeveless black dress which showed off a tattoo of Minnie Mouse on her right shoulder. The dress had a high collar. I couldn't see how short it was because she was sitting down, but I thought it would look good on Lynda.

Mac turned around when I entered. "Ah, Jefferson, I trust you had a productive afternoon."

He was totally ignoring the daggers in my eyes.

"Well, I had a curious incident with the students."

"But there are no students right now," Ralston protested.

"That was the curious incident, Professor." *Zing!*

"Touché, old boy," Mac said heartily. "Hoisted by my own Sherlockian petard! At any rate, you arrive at a timely juncture. Professor Ralston was just propounding a most interesting theory."

"I don't know that I would dignify it by calling it a theory," she protested, standing up. Her dress was knee length. "It's merely a conviction. Good to see you again, Jeff."

While we shook hands, Mac rumbled on. "She believes that Phillimore didn't kill himself."

Taking my cue from Mac, I acted as though this were a totally new notion. "Really? How do you figure that?"

"I've read more than twelve thousand mystery novels, and suicide is never suicide except in the rare instance where it looks like murder but it's really suicide."

I chuckled. "Well, that certainly convinces me, but I think Scotland Yard is going to need a little more to go on."

"There is more, I just can't remember it." Mac cocked an eyebrow. "What I mean is that I almost remember something, but not quite. I've been soaking up all the details of this case, mostly from Faro's articles in *The Daily Eye*. There's something about Phillimore's death that seems familiar. I just can't put my finger on it. But I will."

Mac nodded. "Indubitably. Please let us know when you do."

Ralston leaned back in her chair, arms crossed, considering Mac. "You know Faro, right?"

"We have corresponded for some time. I suppose I could claim to know him to a certain degree."

"Then maybe you can tell me something: He's obviously very plugged in. What does he know about this case that he *isn't* printing?"

"So how was the Silver Fox dressed?" Lynda asked as we sat up in bed reading that night.

"She had a tattoo of Minnie Mouse right here." I pointed to my right shoulder.

"Is that all?"

Incoming, incoming! Should I describe Ralston's apparel in detail or pretend I didn't notice?

"Uh, no, she had clothes on. Let's see. I think she was wearing a black dress." I quickly moved on to relate Ralston's confident assertion that Phillimore had been murdered, a conclusion apparently based on decades of reading mystery fiction. "And then she asked Mac what Faro knows that he hasn't written. Of course, Mac hasn't a clue."

"That's a very interesting question, though. I wonder about that myself, darling. Faro is an American, after all, and Mac thinks an American wrote that suicide text. Two plus two . . ."

I shook my head. "You're getting five. Faro's been writing British English professionally for about fifteen years. He'd never make the mistake of spelling a word American-style."

Solving one mystery in Rome obviously hadn't turned my sweetheart into a super-sleuth.

"I don't like that guy," she said. *No kidding!* "And I connected with some friends of mine on Fleet Street today. They tell me the rumor is that Faro left the U.S. under a cloud all those years ago. It had something to do with stealing voice mail messages to get a story. That bears looking into."

"You should do that."

I closed the book I'd been trying to read, a Max Allan Collins novel. This was the first chance Lynda and I had had to talk about what each of us had done since splitting up. At dinner earlier at Pizza Express, Mac had steered the conversation to Kate's day at the gallery—possibly to avoid reminding me that I was trying to stay mad at him about the King's College debacle. That was fine by me, since my head was ready to explode over the Phillimore case anyway. But Lynda had decided to reopen the subject for pillow talk.

"How did your afternoon go?" I asked.

"Frustrating." Lynda's voice gets huskier at night, which I find by no means unattractive. The rest of her isn't bad either. With an effort of will I ignored my spouse's pajama-clad physical charms and concentrated on what she was saying.

"After I sent in the story questioning whether Phillimore killed himself—with some juicy quotes from Roger to round out Mac's logic—I started trying to contact some of the Phillimore victims on Faro's list. Wow! I almost forgot already what it's like to be on a story where people don't want to talk to you. It's hard to get through to the upper crust types of people who are on the victims list, anyway, and even harder now that they're embarrassed about falling for a con job. So I got a combination of hang-ups and polite promises to take a message. And voice mails, of course. I'll have to go at it again tomorrow."

"Things will look better in the morning," I promised with a yawn, turning out the bedside lamp.

"I had a nap this afternoon, remember? I'm not tired." Lynda leaned over and engaged me in a long, lingering kiss. "In fact, I'm full of energy, *tesoro mio.*"

"Well, what do you know?" I murmured. "All of a sudden, I'm not tired either."

Excerpt from the Professor's Journal
June 11, 2012

*Neville Heath's passion for mystery novels, especially
the works of Sebastian McCabe, makes him the perfect foil.
When McCabe picks up on the clues I've planted, Neville is
smart enough to see the implications that McCabe won't get
until it's too late. Meanwhile, McCabe and his friends are
following one false lead after another. This is starting to be
more fun!*

Chapter Eighteen
Colt .32

"I can't believe we're in London, eating breakfast at a McDonald's," Lynda said the next morning, sipping a cup of caffeine just a few doors away from the King Charles Hotel. "This isn't exactly a health food store, Jeff."

"It's a lot cheaper than the restaurant in our hotel. Besides, this is the new McDonald's. They have Quaker Oat So Simple."

"Sebastian loved the buffet at the hotel," Kate said. "He's going to be out of sorts all day."

Mac arrived about five minutes later, looking not so much out of sorts as distracted.

"What's wrong?" Kate said.

"I have just had a most interesting conversation with Welles Faro," my brother-in-law said, joining us at the table.

"What thrilling new development did he have to report?" Lynda said, acid dripping off of every word.

"According to his sources, someone has reported to Inspector Heath that yours truly owns a .32 Colt revolver, the same kind of gun used to kill Arthur James Phillimore."

I was unimpressed. "Big deal. I could have told Heath that. I even mentioned it in *Holmes Sweet Holmes* and *The* 1895 *Murder.*"

Mac nodded. "Granted. You did *not* tell Heath, however, nor did I. It did not seem relevant. Now some unknown individual has reported this information to

Scotland Yard, apparently with the intention of implicating me in Phillimore's death."

"The plot thickens," I said. Lynda rolled her eyes. *Hey, you have no idea how many years I've waited to say that!*

"Well, that's no problem," Kate said. "You just go to this Inspector Heath and tell him that your gun is back in Erin. It *is*, isn't it?"

"Of course, my dear! Whoever smuggled that illegal weapon into England, it was not I."

Kate looked relieved.

"So what else did old Graybeard have to say?" Lynda asked. Faro's morning story had been an interview with Heath that strongly hinted the Yard wasn't completely satisfied with the suicide narrative. ("The investigation remains open and a cause of death has not been determined.") But the word "murder" wasn't used.

"Welles saw your story on the Grier News Service and asked me to send his congratulations," Mac reported. "He also wondered whether your quotes of Roger Phillimore and Heather O'Toole were accurate. I assured him that they were."

"He'd better not steal them for his column."

"In a not-very-subtle way, he also made it clear that he was already aware of the former romance between Roger Phillimore and his stepmother."

"That's just the sort of thing he would know, isn't it?" I said, beating Lynda to it.

"Indeed. And for that very reason, his treasure house of gossip, I asked Faro to fill me in on the first Mrs. Phillimore. It turns out that she is also an American— Lynette Crosby Phillimore, known as Nettie. Although not well known when Phillimore married her, she was wealthy in her own right. The Crosbys are an old Main Line family. After the divorce, she started a very successful political website known—I regret to report—as *The Net*."

"I'd like to talk to her," Lynda said.

"And I had better talk to Inspector Heath," Mac said.

After breakfast, during which the conversation was restricted to Kate's report on the McCabe children, Mac and Lynda both hit the phones. With a new day came better luck for Lynda. She was able to get an appointment in late afternoon with Mrs. Phillimore the First. Heath told Mac to dash on over.

Lynda went back to the hotel with Kate, saying she wanted to do some Internet research on Nettie and the Crosby clan, while I rode shotgun with Mac to Scotland Yard. I didn't find out until later that Lynda also planned to do a little more shopping.

Heath welcomed us effusively. "Good to see you chaps. Your call quite took me by surprise, Sebastian—may I call you that?"

"Of course, Neville." *The only other people who do are named McCabe, but that's all right. We're all buddies here. I hope.* "As I explained on the telephone, I thought it might be best to discuss this issue of the gun in person. Is it true that someone has reported to Scotland Yard that I own a gun of the same make and model as the murder weapon?"

Prince Charles! That's who Heath reminded me of. That had been nagging at me since we'd first met, but now I had it. The resemblance was in the ears. Heath was probably close to two decades younger than the heir to the throne, but he had the same impressive handles on either side of his long face that I noted in some photos of the Prince.

"At this point we officially don't know that there was any murder, Sebastian," he said. "Nevertheless, I am inclined to think that there was. The autopsy has confirmed the presence of a sedative in the body as well as a good deal of alcohol. That doesn't prove murder, of course, but it is another indicator in that direction."

"But as for any leads that may have come our way, I'm sure you can understand that I'm not at liberty to confirm or deny anything you've heard about that. That just isn't on."

"Of course, Neville, of course. Well, if you haven't received such a report, let me be the first to tell you: I do own such a gun."

"Really?" Heath's ears flew up as he opened his eyes in the pretense of shock. "Well, there's a little surprise. I suppose that slipped your mind during our chat yesterday."

Mac, sitting in a chair in front of Heath, held up his hands as if to distance himself from the notion that he would ever forget anything. "By no means, Neville! It simply never occurred to me that you would be interested. The Colt .32, while perhaps not the most popular firearm, is sold in sufficient quantities as to be unremarkable. When we departed for England, I left my gun in a safe hidden behind a false panel at my home, where my parents are watching our children. If you care to contact Chief Oscar Hummel of the Erin Police Department, I am sure that he would be happy to go to my home and verify that the weapon remains there. You can call him at this cell phone number."

He wrote down Oscar's number on a page of the little notebook he always carries for jotting down plot ideas, tore it out, and handed it to Heath.

Heath sat back. "I might at that, Sebastian. Just as a formality, you understand. I'm sure that if an American killed Phillimore—as you seem to believe—the murderer wouldn't take the risk of bringing the gun with him. Of course, he might take the trouble to acquire the kind of gun he's used to. Although guns of that size are illegal here, they are not unobtainable.

"You know, I've always wanted to write a mystery myself, but I could never come up with a good plot. Do you writer chaps ever base your stories on real life?"

Mac shook his head. "Not I. I find reality much too implausible. I leave the true crime writing to Jefferson and Lynda."

Heath chuckled. "I think I see what you mean. I've had some cases that did strain credulity—stranger than fiction and all that. But might one take some of the circumstances of a real murder and fictionalize it—that is to say, invent a solution that might be quite different than the real one?"

"Of course. It's been done dozens of times with Jack the Ripper alone, sometimes pegging a real historical person as the killer and sometimes using a fictional character."

"Right. So let's see how I'd do at it. Suppose I decided to write a regular whodunit about a world-class swindler who gets murdered. It's made to look like suicide, but our detective sees through that ruse in no time at all."

"Better make your sleuth a Scotland Yard inspector and not an amateur," I said. "You want people to believe it, eh, what?"

Heath ignored me. He kept his eyes on Mac, which only added to the discomfort I was beginning to feel.

"Now, in an Agatha Christie story, or even one of your Damon Devlin adventures, the murderer would never be someone so obvious as one of the victim's cheated clients or one of his wives. It would have to be somebody totally unexpected. Let's see." He stuck a pen in his mouth as if thinking deeply. His acting wouldn't pass muster for a third-grade pageant. "Right, I have it. Brilliant! How about a mystery writer? Has a mystery writer ever murdered anybody?"

"In real life, not just on episodes of *Columbo*?" Mac stroked his beard. "Well, there was a convicted murderer who went on to become a popular mystery writer and is still writing today. However, I do not recall a mystery writer who went on to become a murderer, despite the many temptations afforded in that direction by critics, agents, and publishers. "

"So my ending should be a real shocker! Let's say our murderer is a mystery writer from the States who's never even met the victim until shortly before he kills him."

"Then what's his motive?" I said, liking the direction of this conversation less and less. *I say, Heath, old bean, can we go home to Erin now? I've had quite enough of England, thank you veddy much.*

"Ah, this is the part where I fear it may get a bit far-fetched," Heath allowed. "My fictional mystery writer is an avaricious sort who wants to get his hands on a literary artifact that is absolutely unique—perhaps some sort of journal that the victim has and the murderer wants."

"I think I can see where you got that idea," Mac said. "Did Phillimore's Conan Doyle journal ever turn up?"

Heath shook his head. "No, and we searched Headley Hall, with Ms. O'Toole's permission."

"Well, it is a small item and easily concealed. As a work of fiction, your idea has possibilities. However, it would be a challenge. You would have to first establish that your killer had a mania for collecting." *You mean like those hundreds of mystery books spilling off the shelves in your house and office, Mac?* "Then you would have to make it believable that he—or she—"

"Let's say 'he'," Heath tossed in.

Mac nodded. "—that he is sufficiently psychopathic to take a human life for so slight a gain. I am intrigued by your project, Neville. If you should like me to look at a first draft, I would be delighted to offer my constructive criticism. We mystery writers are always happy to help aspirants in the field, even though they may become our competitors."

Heath was all smiles. "That's very generous of you, Sebastian, very generous indeed. I suppose I should think about an alibi for the killer, but I always think that's overdone in mysteries, don't you? I mean, most people can't prove where they were at any given time. For example, where were you when Mr. Phillimore was killed?"

"I don't know," Mac said smoothly, "because I don't know when he was killed."

"Right. Let's say Sunday morning."

"I was with my wife and the Codys all day."

"From how early?" *Not that early.* Heath waved away his own question. "It hardly matters, chaps. You two are best friends. A cynical sort like the Assistant Commissioner might say that's no alibi at all. That just proves what I was saying—neat alibis are hard to come by in real life."

"I concede your point," Mac said. He actually seemed to be enjoying this joust. I thought it was about as much fun as the flu.

"Well, when you write your mystery based on this case," I said, "make sure the killer isn't somebody who is vastly familiar with English literature and even lived in England for a while and certainly knows how to spell 'honour' the English way like, oh, for instance, Mac."

"Perhaps the killer was in such a hurry that the niceties of correct spelling escaped him," the inspector said.

"But Mac's the one who pointed out the American spelling to begin with!" I hate the way I start to shout when I get excited.

Heath smiled, damn him. "That's just what a clever killer *would* do when he realized his mistake. In fact, isn't that what the murderer did in one of your books, Sebastian? That was *Sleight of Hand*, I believe."

"Quite so, Neville. You must be one of my most attentive fans."

I wish Oscar were on this case. He reads Mac's books, too— just to poke holes in the plots—but I bet he doesn't remember them.

"It's been a right thrill to meet you, Sebastian. In fact, please don't leave London without letting me know."

Chapter Nineteen
The First Mrs. Phillimore

"What the hell was that all about?" I said as we left the Yard. "Heath can't possibly think you really had anything to do with Phillimore's murder!"

Mac lit a Cuban cigar, bought in London. "Indeed, I am not certain that he does, old boy."

I stopped dead. "Then what was the point of that whole interrogation in disguise?"

"Unless I am much mistaken, years of improving his mind with detective stories have imbued Inspector Heath with a very devious turn of mind. Perhaps he suspects that someone is trying to frame me and, in a subtle way, was warning me that this is how the killer intended the circumstantial evidence to be read."

I didn't say anything for a while as I tried to look at that idea from all angles. "After much consideration," I said finally, "I think you're bloody bonkers, to put it in the local lingo. Also barmy and daft! But who am I to say? You're the one who spotted that 'honour' business and figured out that Phillimore might have been drugged. I have to admit that was way smart." *But don't let it go to your head; there's enough going on up there already.*

Mac scowled, an expression not often seen on his bearded face. "Bah! That was child's play. In fact, the ease of it bothers me. Even the missing Conan Doyle notebook seems too pat, the convenient way it sits there just waiting to be hauled out as a motive for yours truly. No, Jefferson, I sense a manipulative hand practically forcing my every move in this case and then turning my own detective work against me."

If I didn't know better, I'd think you were paranoid. But I did know better.

"So what is your—*our*—next move?"

"Lynda has an interview in"—he looked at his Sherlock Holmes wristwatch—"three hours with Lynette Crosby Phillimore. I am sure she would not mind if we tagged along."

"As long as we don't bring Faro with us, I think she'll be fine with that."

We did bring Kate, though, at Lynda's insistence. My artistic sister is an introvert, so I'm not sure she really minded being by herself a lot on this trip, touring galleries alone. But Lynda insisted on feeling guilty about it. So my bride decided that we were going to descend *en masse* on Mrs. Phillimore at her home in Kensington, from whence she operated her profitable website. After a light lunch at a pub near our hotel, we headed for the Charing Cross Station to get on the Underground. Lynda wore a new red dress she'd bought, and carried a matching umbrella. I made a mental note not to let her out of my sight long enough to go shopping again.

On the way, Lynda told us what she'd learned about Roger Phillimore's mother from Internet research and from calls to those journalist friends of hers on Fleet Street.

"The first item of note is that she took more money away from the marriage than she brought to it," Lynda began. "And she used her divorce settlement to start *The Net.*"

"I thought Mac said she came from an old Main Line family," Kate objected. "Doesn't that mean they were wealthy?"

"'*Were*' is the operative word, Kate. Oh, the Crosbys are still rich—Nettie went to Bryn Mawr and all that—but

they're not *really* rich. Think of the Kennedys, a once-great
fortune diminished over the years. What earlier generations
built up, the railroad baron and the hotel magnate, the later
ones were pleased to fritter away as playboys and political
activists. Nettie actually seems to be a kind of late-blooming
throwback to her entrepreneurial ancestors. *The Net* is a big
commercial success—there's even talk that it may go public
or be acquired by one of the big media giants like *The Daily
Beast* and *The Huffington Post* were."

"I had never heard of the site until Faro mentioned
it," Mac said. "Why is it so popular?"

"I guess its political slant appeals to a certain
niche—very left-wing. But my sources tell me the real
popularity driver is Nettie's colorful personality. She pops
up on *The Today Show* and *Good Morning America* all the time,
as well *Daybreak* here in England."

"Is she the woman under the big floppy hat?" I said.

Lynda nodded. "That's the one. I think it's kind of a
marketing gimmick."

Now I remembered her. It seemed to me that Nettie
got hauled out whenever the morning shows were looking
for somebody whose views were slightly to the left of
Vladimir Lenin.

"Apparently Nettie thinks her whole deal is a big
embarrassment to Phillimore, whose politics are way over
on the other end," Lynda said, "and that's why she does it.
At her last birthday—her sixtieth—she had a big bash
attended by like-minded politicos on both sides of the
Atlantic. Even the head of the Labour Party showed up.
Nettie argued with him loudly about British foreign policy.
I'm told that was widely reported in the media, from *The
Daily Eye* to CNN."

With all this intel, I felt well prepped by the time we
arrived at the refurbished Georgian house in Kensington
where Nettie Phillimore maintained both her home and her

office. Although not the size of Headley Hall, it was big enough for several employees to slave away on the ground floor.

A female administrative assistant type, cute but successfully hiding it behind glasses and pigtails, answered the front door. She efficiently led us to Mrs. Phillimore's office beyond a set of double doors. If you didn't know you were in a home, you wouldn't know you were in a home. The square room—probably a former library—was huge and very Fortune 500-looking, but with a touch of elegance provided by real paintings on the walls that would have looked at home in the National Gallery.

Lynnette Crosby Phillimore, sitting at a laptop computer behind her desk and looking dwarfed by her surroundings, couldn't have been taller than about five-five and nicely proportioned. I couldn't guess which Mrs. Phillimore spent more time in the gym, but I bet it was a close thing.

Nettie was dressed in a business-like but not severe tailored suit of blue skirt and jacket, a soft white cotton blouse with a scoop neck, and a simple gold chain necklace. She wore small pearl earrings. Trademark floppy hat nowhere to be seen, her hair was dyed blond and pulled back in a tight bun. Her roots were dark, not gray like Popcorn's. When I shifted my attention to her face, I realized that the full lips and wide eyes seemed familiar. She bore more than a passing resemblance to her successor, but in an older model. As I imagined Nettie with her natural dark hair, the similarity increased. She was still an attractive woman, never mind the mileage.

She looked up from the computer as her administrative assistant announced us and then quickly closed the door behind her.

"Thanks for seeing us," Lynda said.

"I always have time for the news media, honey, but not a lot today," Nettie said, standing up. "I have a guest coming for dinner—and cocktail hour in this house begins promptly at four." *What, no afternoon tea? Oh, yeah. You're an American.* "So you have an hour. I'm asking the first question. Why the hell does it take four people to interview me? Am I that important? And don't try to bullshit a bullshitter because it won't work."

I liked her right away. I could tell from Lynda's smile that she did, too.

"I was hoping you wouldn't mind that I brought my husband and in-laws along," Lynda said. "We're traveling together. This was supposed to be a vacation."

"Supposed to be? You mean before my ex got himself killed?"

"Actually, my vacation kind of ended when your ex disappeared and then his fraud came to light. Grier Media was interested in me reporting on that from the get-go because we don't have a London bureau anymore. Budget cuts."

"You're that Sebastian McCabe, aren't you?" Nettie asked my brother-in-law abruptly.

"Guilty, madam."

"I've been trying to remember where I knew you from. I finally remembered that I saw your picture in *The Daily Eye*. I read that rag religiously, and a damned poor religion it is."

If Nettie hadn't started yapping as soon as we walked in, I'm sure Lynda would have introduced all of us. She did so now as we all sat down in plush chairs.

"You know from *The Eye* that Jefferson and I met your former husband only briefly, the day he disappeared, and Lynda not at all," Mac told Nettie. "You have our sincere sympathy on his passing."

She smiled wryly. "I bet you say that to all his wives." *Well, now that you mention it* . . . "I appreciate your sympathy and I assure you that it's warranted."

Lynda was scribbling like mad. "You were still in love with your former husband?"

Her face did calisthenics as she pondered that one. "Hmm. I haven't really thought about that. But I am sorry that he's not going to spend the next hundred and fifty years in prison, watching me do perfectly well without him." *That sounds plausible.* But it also didn't sound like she'd moved on, as her son had insisted.

Lynda pounced. "Just for the record, did you know that Phillimore Investments was a house of cards, a Ponzi scheme, either during or after your marriage?"

"I'm pretty sure my lawyer would say I shouldn't answer any questions about that because we don't know what my liability might be, or even whether there could be some recovery to investors coming out of my hide." She shrugged. "But I say, 'What the hell.' The lawyer works for me, I don't work for her. So I'll answer. The fact is, I had no idea when we were married that James was involved in funny business. I always thought he was a genius, just like everybody else did." She laughed harshly. "Maybe we thought that because he kept telling us so."

"You said 'when we were married,'" Mac pointed out. "Are we to infer that you learned different after the divorce?"

She sighed. "I might as well tell you that, too. I don't see how it could hurt. I got a call a couple of months ago from a friend of mine, a really smart cookie who had some of his money invested with James. I won't tell you his name, which would be familiar to you, but that doesn't matter anyway. He'd become suspicious because the returns being reported to him were too high for the kind of investments he was supposed to be in. I told him to call Scotland Yard. I don't know for sure that's what brought James down, but I'd like to think so."

"Do you have any idea who would have wanted to kill him?" Lynda asked.

"I've been racking my brains over that one, honey. His demise sure doesn't help me or my son, and I don't know anybody that it would help financially. There must have been another motive, like hatred or revenge. Or maybe he really did kill himself."

Maybe that was it. Maybe Phillimore gave himself a sedative and drank heavily to work himself up to suicide, and maybe the whole drink-and-gun-both-in-the-right-hand thing was a function of somebody disturbing the scene before the crime photos were taken.

But I could see in his deep brown eyes that Mac didn't believe that for a minute.

Nettie's cell phone rang—an irritating flutter up and down the scale. She pulled it out of her pocket and glanced at the name of the caller.

"I'd better take this. Excuse me." I gave her points for the apology.

"Hello, Hillary. Fine thanks. And you? Good. I suppose you want to bitch about my column today? Uh-huh. Well, I didn't expect you to agree, honey. Don't give me that 'real world' bullshit, Hill. If you can't change the real world, what's the point of being a superpower? I disagree, but let's have a few drinks and talk about it when you're in town, okay? You do that. Give Bill my best."

Nettie hung up. "Sorry about that." *Hey, she calls me all the time, too! The woman can't run State without me.*

I hoped my jaw wasn't hanging open. Mac didn't even acknowledge the interruption.

"In my short acquaintance with Mr. Phillimore, he seemed quite an engaging personality," my brother-in-law said. "He also seems to have had the ability to make people believe in him. I suppose that made him both a successful con man and a convincing fiction writer."

"Fiction writer? What do you mean?"

"I guess you wouldn't know that your ex-husband wrote a Sherlock Holmes pastiche for a contest," I explained, just to exercise my vocal chords. "He even won."

She raised her eyebrows. "Really? How about that? James always read a lot, but he never said anything about writing fiction as far as I can remember." Her handsome face took on a wistful look. "When we were young he did write me love letters. He wasn't very good at it, but I didn't care at the time. I still have them somewhere. Maybe that was fiction, too."

Nettie looked at her Cartier watch.

"Thank you very much for your time, Mrs. Phillimore," Lynda said. "We won't cut into your cocktail hour. You've been a great help." *Oh, really?* Nettie was good copy, but if she'd said anything to help find her husband's killer I sure didn't hear it.

"Just don't forget to include the web address of *The Net* in your story—sixteen million hits so far and growing strong."

As we moved to leave, Kate paused by a painting that looked like the cover of a Jane Austen novel, a portrait of a woman with rosy cheeks, an enigmatic smile, and elegant dress, posed against a vague landscape.

"I like your taste in art," Kate told Nettie.

"That's my favorite painting in this room. Sometimes I wonder what she's smiling about, and sometimes I think I know." Nettie smiled herself. "Thanks for the compliment, but my taste has nothing to do with it being here. The art came with the house. I leased the whole shebang as a package from a minor royal who took a drubbing when stocks and everything else fell out of bed in '08. After the divorce, it didn't seem wise to do anything too permanent, like buying a house. But I like it here."

By this time we were at the front door. Nettie opened it to find a find a man poised as if to ring the doorbell. With carefully coiffed light hair, blue eyes, and a blond mustache, he was handsome but a bit short-changed on the height side, being only medium. His black suit fit as if it was made for him, which I'm sure it was.

It took me a few moments to figure out where I'd seen him before, but I had it nailed just before Nettie said, "Oh, hello, Aiden. Right on time." She waived in his direction. "This is Aiden Kingsley, M.P." She hurriedly pronounced our names as well.

"We've met." I said it to Nettie, not to the M.P., so it wouldn't be obvious that I was reminding him of one of those social encounters that public figures are expected to remember and usually don't. "Welles Faro introduced us at the debate Sunday night."

"Oh, yes, of course. Good to see you all again." His upper lip wasn't the only thing that was stiff about him. He was trying hard to be cordial, but the effort was taxing him.

"Aiden is one of the Labour Party's most promising young back benchers." By young, she meant that she had him by about twenty years. *Lynnette Crosby Phillimore, cougar?* I filed that notion under "Possible." "He's also a damned good novelist."

"I especially enjoyed *Abbey Road,*" Mac said. "It may be the best novel about England in the Sixties yet written." *You mean best out of, what, maybe five? This cannot be a big genre.*

"You're very kind." Kingsley was politician-smooth.

"I am particularly interested in the Sixties myself. Perhaps you have read my monograph comparing Don McLean's song 'American Pie' to T.S. Eliot's 'The Wasteland'?"

"Er, not yet. As you might imagine, I was stopping by to offer Nettie my sympathy." *Not to mention knock back a few cocktails, dinner, candlelight, soft music . . .* Sometimes I just don't know when to turn off my imagination. It was getting way ahead of the facts in evidence. I'm sure that Mac could quote something from Sherlock Holmes on that score.

"You've been a good friend, Aiden," Nettie said warmly. *I bet!* There I go again.

The novelist-politician shrugged that off and addressed Mac. "I understand you're making inquiries into this sad business. Any luck?"

"Luck is always a help," Mac said, "but I do not depend on it. So far we have few leads, I am quite pleased to report. 'There is nothing more stimulating than a case where everything goes against you.'"

Kingsley seemed more puzzled than charmed by this bit of contrived paradox. "If you don't mind, then, I'll wish you luck all the same. Sounds like you need it."

Chapter Twenty
The Unsingular Suicide

"I like the way she fessed up about the paintings, not taking the credit for them," Kate said a block or so from the house.

"She does come across as an honest woman, doesn't she?" Lynda said.

"Or somebody trying to seem like one," I added for no particular reason. "What are you thinking, Mac?"

"I am thinking that both of Phillimore's wives, persons who presumably knew him quite well, expressed doubt about his ability to write a piece of fiction."

"And why is that important?" Lynda asked.

"Perhaps it is not. However, it nags at me that 'The Adventure of the Magic Umbrella' not only pointed me toward the priest hole but contained a reference to the singular suicide. The latter is both a chapter title in one of my books and a rather fair description of Phillimore's death. And yet it was supposedly written by Phillimore himself!"

While I was making nothing of that, Mac lit a cigar.

"I am also thinking about the dog that did not bark, metaphorically speaking," he added. "When I threw a quote from Sherlock Holmes at Aiden Kingsley—'There is nothing more stimulating,' etc.— he showed no reaction at all. He is a member of the exclusive Binomial Theorists. Most Sherlockians or Holmesians would be quick to respond by saying, '*Hound of the Baskervilles*, chapter five,' or something of the sort. He did not. I find that puzzling."

I thought he was making a mountain out of a mosquito bite, but I suppressed a snort. "If you say so. The hard fact is that he's sniffing around Phillimore's ex-widow"—*is there such a thing as an ex-widow?*—"just two days after the murder. What do you make of that?"

"Most likely that is mere vulgar intrigue between an ambitious politician and an attractive, albeit older, woman who possesses both wealth and political influence in substantial quantities. Kingsley's novels have been justifiably praised, but neither great fame nor fortune has followed. However, I see no motive for him to kill Phillimore. His name was not on the list of victims; none of the Binomial Theorists were."

I had an answer to that, but before I could give it, Mac's cell phone erupted into *The Ride of the Valkyries*, his oh-so-subtle ringtone.

"Yes? Oh, hello, Professor. Right now? Yes, we have just left the first Mrs. Phillimore. All right, then. We shall see you shortly."

He disconnected. "That was Althea Ralston. She has something to tell us, and she would rather do it in person."

"I'll tag along," Lynda declared. Maybe she wanted to check out the Ralston tattoo. We didn't take a show of hands, but there seemed to be a silent agreement that all four of us would go. It would only be Kate's second visit to King's College. As we boarded the Underground, I picked up the Aiden Kingsley conversation where we had left off.

"He may not have had a reason to do away with Phillimore," I said, "but maybe Nettie wasn't as eager to see old James rot in prison as she claimed. Maybe she wanted to see him six feet under. And maybe her new boyfriend was happy to oblige in return for a lift up in his career, in addition to whatever other favors might be involved."

Hey, that's not half bad! I warmed to my own theory as I talked it out. I was on a roll.

"Kingsley could have been the accomplice who helped Phillimore to disappear. They knew each other from the Binomial Theorists. Suppose Kingsley told him that if he laid low for a while he, Kingsley, could help him get to a country without an extradition treaty with the UK. That would explain how the killer knew he was at the Langham."

"And Nettie knew from her unidentified friend—the investor—that something was rotten in the state of Phillimore, and that Scotland Yard was investigating," Lynda said, speaking rapidly. Excitement grew in her husky voice. She was buying it, at least as an idea with potential. "That gave Kingsley the lever to approach him as a friend wanting to help out. He could have claimed to know about the investigation from his political connections, or even from Assistant Commissioner Madigan."

"But why all the drama of the disappearance?" Kate asked. "Why not just kill him in some simpler way?" That was a question that never would have occurred to her husband, who serves up far more complicated plots in his Damon Devlin mystery novels. "Besides, I think a woman scorned *would* rather see the ex disgraced and imprisoned."

"I am inclined to agree," said Mac. "And yet, I still wonder why the metaphorical dog did not bark."

Althea Ralston awaited us in her office, her usually pale cheeks flushed with excitement. She popped up like a jack-in-the-box when she spotted us through her doorway. This time she was wearing black slacks and a tight-fitting sleeveless mock turtleneck—gray, of course. It struck me that she would have looked right at home in an Emma Peel jumpsuit with lots of zippers and rings.

"I knew there was something I was trying to remember," she said without preamble. No "nice to see you again" for her. "Phillimore's suicide sounded too familiar. Then I remembered a name and I Googled it." She handed

Mac a printout. "This is a news story about a man named Peter Carstairs. He killed himself four years ago in exactly the same way as Phillimore, a gun to the head, at the age of thirty-two. And here's the angle: He was a director, what you would call a vice president, at Phillimore Investments."

"How in the world did you happen to remember a four-year-old suicide of an individual of no particular fame?" Mac asked as he began reading the printout.

"I have an insatiable appetite for violent death."

That shiver I felt down my back wasn't a thrill, at least not any positive kind. *I don't care how nice you are to look at, Professor, I'm glad I didn't take one of your history classes.*

"So what do you think is the connection between the two deaths," Lynda said, "other than the fact that this Carstairs was a Phillimore employee?"

"Isn't it obvious?" Ralston ran a hand through her short white hair, giving the Minnie Mouse tattoo on her shoulder some exercise. Her fingernails were painted black. "He must have caught on to Phillimore's scheme and either asked for blackmail money or told Phillimore he was going to the police. Phillimore had to do away with him."

"Then who killed Phillimore?" I protested.

"He killed himself, using exactly the same technique he used to eliminate the threat from Carstairs. I know I said that he was murdered even before I knew that you and Scotland Yard thought that, but I see now that I was wrong. His conscience must have got the best of him. Even though it's not good mystery form for a suicide to really be a suicide, in this case there's also a murder that everyone thought was suicide. It's brilliant!"

"Well," Mac muttered, "it is at least possible. On the other hand, it could be that a third party killed both Carstairs and Phillimore. There are two people mentioned in this news story that it might be worthwhile talking to— Carstairs's widow and the investigating officer, Andrew Madigan."

Chapter Twenty-One
Fresch Information

"Why would an Assistant Commissioner of the Metropolitan Police Service be investigating a suicide?" I mused aloud as we left King's College.

"He was only an inspector then," Mac explained.

"How convenient that Ralston's solution ties everything up so neatly with the only murderer dead and unavailable for a trial," Lynda said. "Case closed. I wonder what her interest in this is."

"Just being a good citizen, no doubt," I said, like an idiot.

"Subject," Mac corrected. "British nationals are subjects of the Crown, not citizens." *Thanks for the civics lesson, old bean.*

"It's fascinating to see you sleuths at work," Kate said. Sarcasm is a Cody family trait.

Mac looked wounded. *Et tu, Kate?* "I was about to suggest that another discussion with Madigan would be in order. The death of this Peter Carstairs is certainly not something to be ignored."

"I'll call him," Lynda said. "We're practically old friends."

Madigan's phone number was under "Recents" on Lynda's smartphone, but he wasn't in his office. She left a message, telling him that she wanted to talk to him about the apparent suicide of Peter Carstairs four years ago.

"I should also like to speak with Sir Stephen Fresch," Mac said.

That surprised me. "What for?"

"Just a little notion I want to check with him. It should be interesting if it proves out."

"Not to me," Kate said. "This is where I bail. I think I hear another gallery calling my name."

Mac called Sir Stephen, who said he was available for a chin-wag at his office at Stansted. So the rest of us left Kate—with hugs, kisses, and all of that—and headed for the airport.

It was on the way in the Tube that Mac's cell phone serenaded us with *Ride of the Valkyries* again.

"Yes?" Mac boomed, oblivious to the curious looks of our fellow travelers. "Oh, hello, Oscar. It is good to hear your voice."

Apparently he wanted everybody else to hear it, too, because he put the chief on the speakerphone.

"What kind of mess have you gotten yourself into now, Mac?"

"A bloody awful one," Mac said cheerfully. "It's the only kind they have here."

"That I can believe. I got a call about six in the morning from a guy named Heath. Scotland Yard—I couldn't believe it! He didn't seem too sure about me, either. When we got through that, he asked me to go to your house and check out your Colt .32."

"And was it there?"

"Yeah, your dad took me right to it, safely tucked away in a secret panel. Very cute. Now, you want to tell me what's going on?"

Mac looked around. "We are in a rather public place at the moment. I promise to call you back later."

"All right. Tell Jeff I said hi. I owe him an e-mail."

I didn't even get a chance to ask him how Popcorn was before Mac disconnected. Only after the conversation was over did I realize that my overactive imagination had been subconsciously worried that it *had* been Mac's gun that put a bullet in Arthur James Phillimore's brain. I felt more relaxed the rest of the way to the airport.

Poking into the Phillimore caper had taken us to offices at Scotland Yard and in Nettie Phillimore's home. Each had its points, but none was as off-beat as Sir Stephen Fresch's office. It was located in a private jet with the Fresch Air logo on the side.

"Wow, this is something," Lynda said. She snapped a photo of the outside of the plane and immediately posted it to her Facebook page.

Sir Stephen must have been used to explaining his unusual business habitat, because that's what he did as soon as we entered.

"I've never been one to waste pennies on non-essentials," he said, grinning beneath his thick mustache. And this was a guy who spent millions of pounds collecting books and manuscripts of Edgar Allan Poe. "But I needed this office so I can do business even while I'm in the air. Why have another one?"

Why indeed? This one was spacious, wood-paneled, and equipped with all the computers and telephones any executive would need, including the Chief Executive. *Somebody check and see if Air Force One is missing.* There was even a well-stocked bar.

Sir Stephen sat us all down on a comfy couch. After offering us drinks—we all declined, wanting to get down to business—he faced us in a chair with a cup of tea in his hand.

"I hope you don't have to sell this baby because of your Phillimore investments," I said.

If Sir Stephen realized that I was joking, he gave no indication. "The corporation is sound and unaffected by my personal investments. A damned good thing, too. From what my lawyer tells me, the recovery in the Madoff case was minuscule." That faint hint of Eastern European accent got a little stronger. He sipped tea. "But my talk of ruin the other night was just the anger talking. Phillimore held a substantial portion of my wealth that I was willing to put at risk, but not all of it. And there's always my Poe collection if I get down to my last ha-penny."

They don't make the half-penny anymore, but it's still good for a figure of speech.

"It would be sad indeed if you had to part with Poe," Mac said with real empathy. "Vincent Starrett, perpetually strapped for funds, was forced to sell his collection of Sherlockiana. He recreated it, and then had to sell it a second time."

All this Phillimore investment talk had me wondering. "Did you by any chance know a man named Peter Carstairs?" I asked Sir Stephen.

He searched his memory banks and came up blank. "The name doesn't sound familiar. Should it?"

"Perhaps not," Mac conceded. "He was a director of Phillimore Investments. There may have been many. He apparently killed himself four years ago."

"Good heavens! I don't remember that at all. Maybe it happened right before I jumped in. Everybody was buzzing then about what a genius this Phillimore was. Was that what you wanted to talk to me about, McCabe?"

Mac shook his hirsute head. "No, although it was a question worth asking. On Sunday night your reaction to being duped by Phillimore was so strong and so emotional that I suspected your relationship with him was more than just business. So when I called you on the phone today, I asked whether you had known Phillimore well, and you said that you had thought so."

Sir Stephen nodded his bald noggin. "Yes, and you're right, that's what makes this so tough—the sense of betrayal by a friend. We moved in a lot of the same circles—clubs, charities, that sort of thing."

"But not the Binomial Theorists," Lynda put it.

"Oh, no. I'm not a Holmesian. You, of all people, know my preference in detectives, McCabe." He allowed himself a grin of triumphant recollection as he referred to the great debate of Sunday night.

"Indeed. And you know from being present at the debate that Phillimore won the pastiche contest sponsored by the Theorists. Did that surprise you?"

"Very much so."

"He never hinted to you that he was trying his own hand at writing a Sherlock Holmes story?"

"No, just the opposite, in fact. He told me less than a fortnight ago that he could never attempt any such thing. I remember that he was reading a pastiche, *Sherlock Holmes and the Irish Rebels* or something like that. He liked the book and he said he would never even try something like that."

"It seems scarcely credible that he would then go on to write an accomplished short story within a few days," Mac observed. "As a mystery writer of some experience, I can assure you that Sir Arthur Conan Doyle was not far wrong when he said that a short story takes as much effort to write as a novel. The plotting is not as easy as it looks to a non-writer. Are you absolutely certain that you remember correctly the time frame when he made this comment?"

"Easy enough to check." Sir Stephen pulled out his smartphone and accessed his calendar. "The benefit dinner for the Homeless Aid Society was held on May 30. That's the last time I saw him, and I'm sure that's when we had the conversation I recall. What does that have to do with anything?"

"That remains to be seen," Mac rumbled, "other than the obvious fact that Phillimore did not write the pastiche submitted to the contest under his name. He lacked the time and inclination, as well as the talent. The deadline for submitting entries to the contest was Thursday, June 7, the day Phillimore disappeared—a very late deadline because the contest was announced late. I read the five entries the following day. "

Lynda stopped scribbling and looked up from her notebook. "You could have asked Faro about this. He probably knew Phillimore a lot better than Sir Stephen did. But you didn't want him to know what you're up to and print it, did you?"

Mac beamed. "That is an excellent deduction, Lynda! The story is all yours, when the time is right. You will recall that, in his role with the Binomial Theorists, Faro collected the manuscripts for the contest and then forwarded them to me and the other judges. When I read 'The Adventure of the Magic Umbrella' with its Phillimore-centric plot after the disappearance of Arthur James Phillimore, I prevailed on Faro to tell me the name of the author. If he did not then see reason to suspect the authenticity of the story's authorship, it is certainly not my responsibility to raise the issue with him." *So the McCabe–Faro hatchet hasn't been buried after all! Not that Lynda minds.*

A detail bothered me. "How were the stories submitted?"

"By e-mail," Mac said.

"That's what I would have thought. Shouldn't Faro have noticed that it didn't come from Phillimore's e-mail address?"

Lynda snorted, the cutest little snort in the world. "Assuming he even paid attention to the address, how many of your friends have changed their e-mail addresses multiple times? For that matter, how many maintain more than one account with different providers?" *Counting me?*

The question was rhetorical, so I didn't answer.

"This is all quite a puzzle, isn't it?" Sir Stephen said. "Perhaps you should look to Poe for the answer. You might find it hiding in plain sight."

Chapter Twenty-Two
Faro

"Okay," Lynda said as we left the hangar, "what does it mean that Phillimore didn't write that story?"

"It means," said Mac, "that I was right in this feeling that I have been manipulated. The murderer wrote that story, knew that I would read it, and wanted me to pick up the clue that led me to the priest hole. Even the reference to the 'singular suicide' in the story seems aimed at me, given my chapter title of that name."

"But why?" I said.

"I can only surmise that the point was to draw me into the case, at first a disappearance but now a murder in which a certain amount of circumstantial evidence points back at me. In short, I do not think the murderer likes me very much."

Never overlook the obvious.

"Okay, I can buy it," Lynda said, "but I'm not so sure that my editors at Grier will."

"No, what we have garnered from Sir Stephen, although helpful to me, is rather thin gruel for responsible journalism," Mac acknowledged. "That is by no means unfortunate from my point of view. I would rather the world, including the murderer, not know just yet that we are on to the true authorship of the pastiche and its purpose."

"Speaking of responsible journalism," Lynda said, "here comes the opposite."

The portly, bearded figure of Welles Faro was heading our way, waving his hand to attract our attention.

"He will certainly ask questions," Mac said. "I suggest that we be circumspect with our answers."

"You don't have to tell me," Lynda said. "In fact, maybe if I ask him enough questions he won't be able to get in any." *That's a good plan, Lyn, except for the fact that it won't work. I'm sure that Faro on the track of a story is about as easy to sidetrack as you are.*

"Hello, chaps," Faro said when he got close enough. "What a surprise."

"It sure is," Lynda said. "What are you doing here?"

Faro's hairy face split in a grin. "I'm always somewhere. What about you?"

"Just getting a little fresh air," I quipped.

"Yes, I know the hangar," Faro said dryly.

"Tell me, Welles, do you plan to write about this nonsense regarding the murder weapon?" Mac asked.

"I already have, my dear fellow. It will go up on the website shortly. Come now, I could scarcely ignore it for friendship's sake! It was an interesting bit of news concerning a very high profile case."

"But Heath has already checked it out and confirmed that Mac's gun is at his house!" Lynda blurted out.

"Oh, really? Thanks for the tip. Still, the whole thing is interesting, don't you think? I'm sure you'll be writing about the gun as well, Ms. Teal." *No, she won't.* "I've been following your stories on the Grier wire from the beginning. They've been very well done indeed. I congratulate you." *That's the most dismissive congratulations in history, Faro. Congratulations!*

"Of course the murder weapon wasn't yours, Professor McCabe," he went on. "I'm sure Heath realizes the fact that you own a gun of the same type as the murder weapon is just one of those odd occurrences that Holmes said happen when you have a few million people jostling around together. It's silly to think that you would have anything whatever to do with Phillimore's demise."

He looked from one to the other of us, maybe trying to see if anybody took his bait. When no one did, he continued. "I understand from my sources at the Yard that the missing Conan Doyle notebook hasn't turned up yet. Did you know that?"

"You might be surprised what we know," Lynda said. "Were you one of Phillimore's investors?"

"Me? Of course not. I don't have that kind of money. Why do you ask?"

"Asking questions is just a habit I have, being a journalist and all. I thought maybe you forgot to include yourself on the list of victims you published in *The Daily Eye*."

"Don't be fooled by the wealthy company I sometimes keep, Lynda. I was taken in by James, just like everyone else, but I am not a man of means, and certainly not one with excess funds to invest. What did Nettie have to say? Does she have any ideas about the death of her ex?"

"Why don't you ask her?" Lynda said.

"So you did talk to her! Maybe I'll pop around and have a chat with her as well. She didn't happen to confess to killing her husband, did she? Well, I understand if you prefer not to say. I'm sure I'll read about it on the Grier wire. I can't help noticing that your group is not complete. Where is the lovely Mrs. McCabe?"

"Let us say she is engaging in researches of her own," Mac said.

Faro tutted. "That's not good. You should be enjoying London together—take in a play or something like that."

"Would that I could, Welles! This working vacation has turned out to be more work than vacation, although little of it has had to do with St. Benignus College."

"Well, I won't keep you," Faro said, beginning to move away.

"Give Sir Stephen our regards," Lynda said.

She was still fuming after Faro disappeared into the hangar. "I feel like he's stalking us," she said. "He knew from his phone conversation with Mac this morning that we were going to talk to Heath and Nettie Phillimore. I get that. But how did he find out that we would be calling on Fresch? I didn't even know until right beforehand. It's sure hard to get a leg up on Faro."

"But you did," I said, "thanks to Althea Ralston. If Faro knows anything about the suicide of Peter Carstairs, he didn't give a hint of it."

"That's right!" Lynda bit a lip thoughtfully. "The question is, do I go with that angle now or wait and see if I can get a stronger story by talking to Carstairs' widow?"

"I'd wait," I said. "You're not going to lose the story to Faro, and you haven't written about Heather O'Toole yet."

"Heather didn't say much that I could use."

"Perhaps you could add interest by combining that material with your Nettie Phillimore interview," Mac said. He waved his hand in front of him as if envisioning a headline. "'**A TALE OF TWO WIVES**.' How does that sound?"

"Like a *Daily Eye* headline," Lynda said. "But I get your point: There's something to be said for fighting fire with fire."

Excerpt from the Professor's Journal
June 12, 2012

I didn't expect the red herring about McCabe's gun to collapse so soon. But no matter. I've managed to plant a seed of doubt and suspicion with Heath. That's all I need. I'll be leaving this game soon anyway.

Chapter Twenty-Three
The Widow Carstairs

"We are going to the theater this afternoon," Mac announced at breakfast the next morning at our hotel.

"Why are we doing that?" I asked.

"Not 'we' as in you included, T.J." Kate told me with an unseemly cheerfulness. "We as in 'Mac and me.'" *Don't look at me like that, sis! It was your idea to turn my honeymoon into a vacation for four.*

"Faro had some young minion—one of his vaunted Fleet Street Irregulars, I presume—drop off a pair of tickets to today's matinee of *Cloak and Dagger* at the Oliver Cromwell Theatre on St. Martin's Lane," Mac explained. "A generous gesture, no doubt, but galling in its assumption that we have nothing better to do at three o'clock."

"We don't," Kate said firmly.

"Wow, that play's been running five years in the same theater," Lynda said. "It may eventually outlast *The Mousetrap*. I'd love to see it some time."

I kicked her gently under the table, just to get her attention. "Some time, sure." She was getting dangerously close to looking a gift horse in the mouth.

After a murderous look at me, Lynda announced, "I found Margaret Carstairs."

"Who?" Kate said.

"The widow of the man who supposedly killed himself four years ago in a manner quite similar to

Phillimore's departure," Mac said. "I told you about it last night. You hung on my every word."

"Oh, that Margaret Carstairs."

"Anyway," Lynda said rather heavily, trying to get the conversation back on track, "I found her phone number online and I called her this morning. As you might imagine, she was taken aback when I started talking about her husband being murdered. But when she got over the shock, she said, 'I knew it' and started crying. She agreed to meet us at ten o'clock at her favorite Starbucks in Mayfair."

Mac turned pale at the mention of the global coffee chain, transparently considering it insufficiently English, but he merely said: "I salute your enterprise, Lynda. Well done!"

That wasn't the only thing she'd done before breakfast. She'd also taken advantage of the hotel's free WiFi to run an Internet search on Aiden Kingsley. His name popped up about every other day on *The Net*, invariably with superlative adjectives attached. Nettie found him "brilliant," "savvy," "charming," "handsome," "astute," "up-and-coming," and "energetic." Whether her fascination was political or personal, Lynette Crosby Phillimore was definitely besotted with her favorite backbencher.

I was still chewing on that when we set off to meet Margaret Carstairs. It turned out that she worked as an estate agent and didn't have a showing until one o'clock. Kate opted out of the venture, heading instead for the Tate Britain gallery.

About a block from the address we'd been given, Mac's cell phone went off. It's always amusing to see the reaction to *Ride of the Valkyries* on a crowded street. Mac pulled out the phone and looked at the screen, which he usually forgot to do. "It's Inspector Heath," he announced before putting the phone to his ear.

"Hello, Neville. How may I help you? No, never. I am quite certain. Why do you ask? All right. Good-bye."

He disconnected. "That was most curious. Inspector Heath asked me if I have ever exchanged e-mail with Arthur James Phillimore."

"What's up?" Lynda asked.

"He said he may be able to tell me later."

Margaret Carstairs had told Lynda to look for "the gal in the white straw hat." That made it easy to spot her as soon as we walked in the door. She was a plump, attractive woman in her mid-thirties with shoulder-length auburn hair sticking out of the hat. Her dress was a kaleidoscope pattern of yellow, orange, and white. She was reading *The Daily Eye*.

The lead headline of the paper was ragging on the Prime Minister for forgetting his young daughter in a pub after a night on the town. Faro, as promised, had unloaded his story about Scotland Yard investigating a tip about the Colt .32 that killed Phillimore. Lynda's piece about the two Mrs. Phillimores, picked up by Grier News Service clients around the world, had a softer edge but I thought it was more interesting to read than a tale of a lead that went nowhere. Faro also had a small sidebar about Heather O'Toole returning to the set of *Dragonfly* in Barbados.

"Mrs. Carstairs?" Lynda said.

"Oh!" She looked up from the paper, startled, as if she'd been concentrating. She had striking green eyes. "Yes, I'm Margaret Carstairs." She stood up, smoothing her dress with her hands. She stood about five-seven, taller than the average American woman but shorter than most of the women in my life.

"I'm Lynda Teal. Thank you for seeing us. This is my husband, Jeff Cody, and his brother-in-law, Sebastian McCabe."

"You were with him when he disappeared, weren't you? Mr. Phillimore, I mean." She went on without waiting for an answer. "I've read all the stories in the newspaper. I was interested because Peter worked for Mr. Phillimore."

"And they died in very similar ways," Lynda said. "That's what caught our attention. You said on the phone that you always knew your husband had been killed."

She sat down next to Mrs. Carstairs while Mac and I arranged ourselves on the other side of the table.

"I tried to tell the police." Mrs. Carstairs sipped her cup of coffee. "They thought I was just a silly woman, hysterical because my husband was dead and I had a bun in the oven. But I knew Peter would never leave our baby and me."

"How did it happen?" Lynda said, managing to infuse those four words with a world of empathy. "I know that this must be very painful for you. I wouldn't open up these wounds, Mrs. Carstairs, if I didn't think it might help."

"You're not opening any wounds. They were never closed." She took a deep breath and another gulp of java. "I came home for lunch one day after showing a house. I expected to be alone because Peter never came home for lunch. I happened to be walking by his den and I noticed that the door was standing open. He usually kept the door closed because it was messy in there, so I peeked in."

Margaret Carstairs looked like she needed something a lot stronger than caffeine, but she kept talking. I give her full points for not giving in to the sobs that were lurking. "His body was on the floor and there was a lot of blood. He'd been shot through the head."

Lynda put her arm around the widow. "I'm so sorry."

"Thank you."

"According to a news story I read, the weapon was a .22 target pistol," Mac said. "Did your husband belong to a gun club?"

"No, he didn't even own a gun. He hated guns."

"Even the .22 is illegal under British law unless the owner belongs to a gun club," Mac mused. "He would have had to have acquired it illegally."

"You see? Peter would never do such a thing. He was a law-abiding citizen." *That's "subject," not "citizen."* But it didn't seem like the time to correct her.

"People sometimes act out of character when they're having a problem," Lynda said, "even to the point of killing themselves. Had he been depressed or otherwise acting strangely?"

"No, he—" She stopped. "Nobody ever asked that question because they thought I was just daft, so I never thought about it until now. He wasn't depressed, but I did think there was something on his mind. He seemed preoccupied. I thought maybe he was just a little nervous about the baby coming. But one night—probably less than a week before he died—I finally said to him, 'Is something bothering you, Peter?' And he said, 'Not anymore. It's about work, but I've made up my mind what to do. I'm going to tell someone.'

"A couple of days later, he seemed more like his old self, so I said to him, 'Well, Peter, did you have that talk?' He knew right away what I meant, and he said yes, and it was going to be, quote, 'a big story.'"

"Did he say anything more about the matter?" Mac pressed.

Mrs. Carstairs shook her head, giving the big hat a workout. "Not that I recall."

"He said it was about work," Lynda pointed out. "I'm sure you've read all about the collapse of Phillimore Investments and the investigation of the Ponzi scheme there."

"Yes, and I was totally shocked. Obviously, I had no idea."

"But do you think Peter did? Could that be what was bothering him?"

Her perfectly penciled eyebrows shot up. How this thought had apparently never occurred to Margaret

Carstairs before now, I could not fathom. "I suppose it's possible. He was a director, so perhaps he would have been in a position to know if there was something crooked about the company. But Mr. Phillimore was so kind and so generous to me and Peter Jr.—Repete, I call him. Truly, the man couldn't have been nicer."

Guilty conscience? Maybe Ralston was on to something with her idea that Phillimore whacked Peter Carstairs, but then felt so bad about it that he killed himself in a similar way. But wait—the gun didn't fit in with that. The fact that Phillimore was killed with the same kind of gun that Mac owns didn't mean that Mac had anything to do with it, but it must mean something. I didn't think it meant that Phillimore wanted to implicate Mac—whom he'd met exactly once—on his way out of this life.

"Why do you think the police failed to take your concerns seriously?" Mac asked.

Mrs. Carstairs shrugged. "They already had a storyline and they weren't looking for another one. And they believed the text."

Mac raised an eyebrow. "Text?"

"Peter supposedly sent me a farewell text from his cell phone. I'll never forget the words: 'Good-bye, Margaret. Please forgive me. I'll see you on the other side.'" She looked at Lynda. "Bollocks!" I later found out that this is a Britishism for *nonsense*. "Peter didn't write that. Like I told that man from Scotland Yard, my hubby never called me 'Margaret' in his life. 'Maggie' was his name for me."

Chapter Twenty-Four
Death in the Afternoon

"Some vacation!" I complained on the way back to the King Charles Hotel. "I'm wrung out."

"I know what you mean," Lynda said. "Listening to that poor woman was emotionally exhausting. I need some down time in our room." My ears perked up. This sounded very appealing to me. "I think I'm on to a hell of scoop," my dear spouse went on. "But I suppose you're going to tell me I shouldn't write it, Mac."

"Not yet, please," he said. "We are on the trail of someone who has killed at least twice. The earlier instance of a suicide note by text message, cleverly avoiding the sticky issue of the deceased's handwriting, ties the two cases together unmistakably. At this point, the killer should have no idea that we know that. That advantage is not one to be tossed away."

Lynda sighed. "Well, I need to talk to somebody from Scotland Yard first, anyway—preferably Assistant Commissioner Madigan." He still hadn't returned her phone call asking for an interview about the Carstairs case.

Back at the hotel, Mac went to his room to meet up with Kate and go to the matinee. Lynda and I . . . well, we were still on our honeymoon.

It was some time after three o'clock—I didn't look at the bedside clock—when Lynda's cell phone rang, dragging me out of a deep sleep. I felt like a punch drunk boxer who hears the bell and can't figure out where that strange noise is coming from. Lynda, being made of stronger stuff, immediately reached over and answered the pesky device. Even with her honey-colored hair in disarray she was a bonny lass.

"Yes, this is she." She sat up. "Oh, hello, Welles." She made a gagging motion with her finger down her throat. I reached up and tried to distract her. She swatted my hand away, but I like to think her heart wasn't really in it. "Yes, but how did you . . . I see. Well, that's very generous of you. I appreciate it." She had a pained look on her oval face as she choked the words out. "What's the address?" She grabbed a hotel pen and pad from the night stand. "Okay. Got it. We'll be there. Thanks again."

She disconnected and threw the cell phone on the bed. "That was the enemy," she said unnecessarily as she pulled on her bright red unmentionables. *Hey, don't get dressed on my account.* "I don't believe this. Madigan never bothered to call me back, but when Faro called him he told that scoundrel that he'd talk to both of us at the same time. He wants us to meet him at his house in Upper Norwood at four o'clock."

"That's odd."

"It sure is. And why would Faro go along with letting me in on this? He must have an angle."

"Maybe he just likes you. I certainly do, my sweet." My attempts to demonstrate this were gently rebuffed with the removal of my hands and the suggestion that I put some clothes on. Reluctantly, I did so.

Madigan's place was a Victorian-era brick detached house on a leafy street. Faro was waiting for us on the porch when we arrived from the Tube station, a thick volume called *The Napoleon of Crime* under his arm.

"This is really nice of you," Lynda said sweetly. "I don't imagine you do many joint interviews."

Faro bowed theatrically, no easy trick for a man of his waist size. "Consider it a favor to a fellow American, my dear lady. Besides, Andy insisted."

"You're friends, of course," I said. *As in, he's your main pipeline into Scotland Yard.*

"Of course. We go way back."

He pushed the doorbell. We could hear it ring inside the house. We waited, but the door didn't open. Faro was just about to push the bell again when we heard another noise—a loud pop, like a firecracker.

"That was a pistol shot!" Faro exclaimed.

He turned the door handle and pushed. Surprisingly, it opened.

We stood at the threshold, looking at each other. "This can't be good," Lynda said finally.

With Faro in the lead, we moved forward together into the house.

The door opened into a hallway, tastefully furnished with a combination hat rack and wooden bench on one wall and a seascape painting on the other. Not dawdling, we kept going until we came to a small home office at the back of the house.

Lynda squeezed my right hand in a death grip. Assistant Commissioner Andrew Madigan's body was sprawled on the floor, his life's bright red blood pouring out onto an oval area rug. He held a gun in his lifeless hand.

Chapter Twenty-Five
Echoes of Birlstone

"This may be a first," Heath said about an hour later, looking down at the body. "I don't believe we've ever lost an assistant commissioner before. Not this way, I mean."

He knelt down and, wrapping the gun in his handkerchief, lifted it up to his nose.

"You'll never convince me he killed himself," I said.

Heath chuckled. "No, there's not a chance of that. This gun hasn't been fired. Also, he was probably shot from a distance, judging by the lack of puckering on the flesh at the entry wound on his chest. The killer seems to have left by the back door, which is wide open."

"Is that his service weapon?" Faro asked.

"That's right, sir—Glock 26 semi-automatic, 9mm."

Charming detail.

"Something tells me the murder weapon was a Colt .32," Heath added dryly.

The Madigan domicile was already crawling with police. We'd called Heath directly as soon as we'd established that Madigan was as dead as he looked. The inspector had unnecessarily told us to stay put and not touch anything. But he didn't tell us not to contact Mac. I sent my brother-in-law a text that began, *You won't believe this, but . . ."*

"I thought I was under a lot of pressure before, what with Mr. Roger Phillimore calling me two or three times a day," Heath said, standing up. "This is going to make my life hell. Let's take it from the top. What are you three doing here?"

"In my case, the possible murder of a man named Peter Carstairs," Lynda said.

"What?" With ears his size, I figured that Heath had heard her, he was just having trouble processing it. So Lynda and I, basically by turns but occasionally tripping over each other, gave him the lowdown on Althea Ralston's tip about Peter Carstairs and our interview with his wife.

"And since Madigan was the investigating officer, we thought maybe he could tell us something," Lynda said.

"For instance," I added, "why did Scotland Yard apparently never take a serious look at Mrs. Carstairs's insistence that her husband didn't kill himself?"

Heath looked thoughtful—or clueless. How was I supposed to know what that look meant?

"And you, sir?" he said to Faro.

The Anglo-American drew himself up to his full five-six or so. "I heard rumors of a new angle on the Phillimore fraud. I tried to pry the facts of it out of Andy, and he told me to meet him here. But he insisted that he would only talk to me and Ms. Teal at the same time."

"I thought you were buddies," Lynda said. She's so cute when she's being a hard ass.

"Indeed we were." He held up the book in his hand, *The Napoleon of Crime.* "In fact, I was planning to lend him a book that I thought he might enjoy. I often did that. Our friendship was the very reason he didn't want to give me an unfair journalistic advantage."

What a load of crap, Faro. Lynda had a scoop on Peter Carstairs until you were invited to the party. My beloved held her tongue, but her gold-flecked eyes were on fire.

"But isn't it true that Assistant Commissioner Madigan was your inside source at the Yard, sir?" *Way to go, Heath, old bean!*

Faro tried to look dignified, which is hard when the cuffs on your sport coat come down longer than they should. "I don't reveal my sources, Inspector."

"That's as may be, sir, but I know that you've published a lot about the Phillimore case—too much, I'd say—that you didn't get from me. The thought occurred to me that perhaps the Assistant Commissioner was killed for that very reason."

That got a rise out of Faro. "I very much doubt that, Inspector. But in any case, I still can't talk about my sources. It's a matter of ethics."

Lynda appeared just on the verge of lobbing a suitably acerbic rejoinder Faro's way when the doorbell rang, startling all of us.

The cop who answered the door did a darned good imitation of Trout, or even Jeeves. "I'm sorry, sir, you can't come in here; this is a crime scene."

"Quite understandable," came a familiar rumble in reply. "However, I am quite sure that Inspector Heath will be interested to know that Sebastian McCabe is at the door."

"Let him in, Hawkins," Heath yelled down the hallway. "What's a circus without a ringmaster?" he added under his breath.

Mac bustled in, with Kate right behind him. She looked like she'd rather be at a Laundromat at midnight.

"Hello, Sebastian," Heath greeted. "You're just in time to hear my star witnesses tell me about their discovery of the body."

Mac nodded wordlessly in acknowledgement.

"I arrived first," Faro began. He told most of the story, with Lynda and me chiming in with a detail or two. It didn't take long.

"Did the neighbors see or hear anything?" Mac asked.

"We're still knocking on doors to ask about that," Heath said. "Where were you during this time?"

"Kate and I were at the Oliver Cromwell Theatre, seeing *Cloak and Dagger*. It is a highly overrated melodrama, in my opinion."

"I loved it," my sister said.

Heath shook his head mournfully, looking uncannily like a Bassett hound who had just heard bad news. "Not much of an alibi, is it? Of course your wife would back you up, Sebastian. And even if she's on the up and up you might have left her for a few minutes."

"Hell and damnation," Mac thundered, "you cannot possibly believe—"

"And I don't," Heath said. "But someone wants me to. This morning I received what was alleged to be a series of e-mail exchanges between you and Phillimore in which you alternately attempted to threaten and cajole him into selling you that Conan Doyle notebook. He refused. Supposedly, the anonymous person who sent it to me was inspired to come forward by reading about that Colt business in *The Daily Eye*." Heath glanced at Faro, who didn't have the conscience to look embarrassed.

"Ingenious!" Mac said. He stuck an unlit Cuban cigar in his mouth.

"Too clever by half, I'd call it," Heath said. "The two e-mail addresses that were supposed to be you and Phillimore looked plausible enough, but through only slightly illegal means I was able to establish that both were created on the same day—one Yahoo and one Gmail. Someone went to a great deal of trouble to write both ends of that e-mail thread."

"This is dynamite!" Faro exclaimed.

Lynda rolled her eyes.

Heath held up his hands as if fending off an objection that no one had spoken. "I've read enough of your books, Sebastian, to know that in a novel that might be a double bluff. You could have framed yourself. But I don't see you taking that chance. And I don't see you killing Mr. Phillimore to get that notebook."

"I quite agree, Neville," Mac said heartily. He looked down at the body. "And Phillimore was only one of the victims. Madigan makes three."

Heath raised his eyebrow. He only had one, all the way across. "Three?"

"Surely that is self-evident? No doubt a Scotland Yard official might accumulate many enemies in the course of a career, even murderous ones. However, following so closely the murder of Arthur James Phillimore, a man that Madigan knew on a social level, it is hard to believe that this death is not related to his."

Heath ostentatiously held up his index finger and then his middle finger. "Phillimore, now Madigan, and I presume the third, or really the first, was this Peter Carstairs that Ms. Teal was telling me about."

"Precisely—Carstairs, Phillimore, Madigan." Mac stopped dead, stoking his beard. "Unless the second dead man wasn't Phillimore!"

"What do you mean by that?" Faro demanded. I'm pretty sure he was only a half-step ahead of Lynda with that question.

"I'm thinking back to 'The Adventure of the Magic Umbrella' and its reference to the Sherlock Holmes stories with hidden rooms," Mac explains. "In both of those stories, 'The Adventure of the Norwood Builder' and *The Valley of Fear*, the supposed murder victim is actually still alive. Suppose that Phillimore faked his own death and then killed Madigan out of revenge for his role in bringing down Phillimore Investments!"

"But you said Phillimore didn't write the short story," Lynda pointed out.

So there!

Mac frowned.

"Ms. O'Toole did give a positive identification of Phillimore's body, Sebastian," Heath pointed out.

The best Mac could come up with by way of a comeback was, "Hmmm. Perhaps you had better run a fingerprint comparison anyway, Neville. I assume that no one thought that was necessary until now."

"I still don't think it is," said Heath amiably, "but I'll do it." He looked down at the corpse. "At least there's no question about who *he* is. I don't look forward to informing Mrs. Madigan. I've met her." He gave a theatrical shiver.

One of Heath's troops stuck his head in the doorway. "Excuse me, Inspector."

"What is it, Weedly?"

"I finally found a neighbor, a retired schoolteacher across the street who was out in his yard. He heard what must have been the fatal shot a little more than an hour ago. He said he didn't think much of it because he heard a whole string of similar pops not long before. He thought it was some kids with fireworks."

"Didn't see anything suspicious beforehand?"

"No, but he said he wasn't looking. He said he's not, quote, 'one of those old people who becomes a nosy-parker.'"

Heath snorted. His snort wasn't nearly as cute as my beauteous bride's.

"Thanks, Weedly. Keep at it."

While they were talking, Mac had walked over to Madigan's desk. "This is interesting," he muttered, without looking up. "In Poe's best detective story, 'The Purloined Letter,' an important letter is 'hiding in plain sight,' as Sir Stephen Fresch and many others have put it. It's in a card rack, perhaps something like this." Mac reached into what I would have called a letter rack and pulled out an envelope.

"I couldn't help but notice the Langham Hotel return address. It's postmarked on Monday."

He handed it to Heath.

I don't know what UK law says about opening the mail of a dead man, but if any solicitors are reading this I ask you to close your eyes.

Actually, the envelope had already been slit up at the top. Heath just pulled out the contents.

Not surprisingly, the piece of paper inside was a sheet of Langham Hotel stationery. A series of numbers were written on it in ink:

254-16-1
197-6-15
531-10-9
770-7-10

"What the hell?" Lynda said. *My thoughts exactly, my love.* We were both being obtuse, of course. Mac tried to act like he wasn't talking to half-witted children, but failed utterly, as he said, "It's a cipher, of course, right out of Sherlock Holmes."

"*The Valley of Fear*," Faro said, almost automatically.

"I've read it," Heath said, "but it's been years. I'm afraid I'm a little rusty on my Holmes." He looked at Faro in silent appeal.

"It's in the first chapter, Inspector," Faro said. "Holmes gets a cipher message from one Fred Porlock, his informant inside Professor Moriarty's gang. Porlock has sent the message, but then, in a panic because he knows that Moriarty suspects him, decided not to send the key to the cipher. In a piece of brilliant logic, Holmes deduces that the numbers in the cipher refer to the page numbers, columns and words of a particular book—*Whitaker's Almanack* for the year in which the adventure took place."

As Faro spoke, Mac scanned the titles in the modest built-in bookcase opposite Madigan's desk.

"No *Whitaker's* here," he commented.

"Did you really expect there would be?" Lynda asked.

"I own a *Whitaker's Almanac* of 1888"—*I am shocked, SHOCKED!*—"and I suspect that I am far from alone. Assistant Commissioner Madigan, however, apparently owned only one Sherlock Holmes book. That strikes me as quite extraordinary. Even non-collecting Sherlockians and Holmesians inevitably acquire several different editions and a few related books. Fortunately, Madigan's one book is all we need."

He pulled a fat paperback off the shelves, *The Penguin Complete Sherlock Holmes*. I'd seen one just like it a few days ago at Scotland Yard.

"Phillimore had a copy of that same edition with him at the Langham!" Heath said with some excitement.

"Quite so," Mac said. "That is why this book is all we need. "May I see that sheet of paper?"

"That's probably the most commonly owned edition of the Canon in the UK," Faro said as Heath handed the paper to Mac. "This has to be a setup of some kind. It's too pat. The killer planted that message."

"If that is so," Mac said, "it would be ungrateful indeed for us not to unwrap the gift. With the key in hand, that should be simplicity itself. Since the only large numbers are at the beginning of the groups of three, I hypothesize that the first number is the page, the second is the line, and the third is the word in that line. What do we get when we try that?"

Mac looked at the numbers, memorized them, and started looking them up.

"Page two hundred fifty-four, line sixteen, the first word is 'don't.' That sounds promising! This could be a warning." He paged quickly to the next set of numbers. "'Trust'! The warning tone continues." Mac flipped more pages. "'The.' What a disappointment! I was hoping for a name. Instead we get 'Don't trust the—' He found the last word, held his finger on it and looked up. "'Professor.' The message is: 'Don't trust the professor.'"

"Maybe he should have taken that advice more seriously," Lynda said.

Chapter Twenty-Six
The Professor

"Did you notice how Faro lost no time in pointing out that Mac's a professor?" Lynda said during dinner that night at a pub around the corner from our hotel. "I can't wait to see how he uses that in his column. What a sleazebag." *The love fest continues.* Lynda had already written and filed her story.

"You don't think that Inspector Heath took that seriously, do you?" said Kate, in a tone that suggested she feared exactly that.

"Neville is a canny one, a bit hard to read," Mac said. "In our dealings with him, however, he has amply demonstrated that he is hardly the dullard that Scotland Yard inspectors are portrayed in the Canon and in other mysteries. And surely only a dullard could believe that Phillimore would write a coded message to Madigan—a man I barely knew—telling him not to trust me. What would he have to trust me or not trust me about? Besides, I am not commonly known as 'the Professor.'" I'm going to capitalize it like that whenever the title refers to a specific person, identity unknown.

Mac went back to shoveling in the bangers and mash.

"So, do you think the cipher was another false clue, part of a ham-handed effort to frame you?" I asked, looking up from my fish cakes.

"It is certainly possible. The killer could have planted the books at both murder scenes. However, if the wording of the message were designed to implicate me, would it not have been far more direct? For example, there is a reference to 'Mr. Mac' in *The Valley of Fear* that could have been used, perhaps coupled with the 'Sebastian' of Sebastian Moran in 'The Adventure of the Empty House.'"

Mac paused. "I still find it more than passing strange, by the way, that Madigan apparently owned only one Sherlock Holmes book and yet he belonged to the most elite group of Holmesians in London."

"So does that politician, Kingsley, and he didn't respond to the quote you threw at him as we were leaving Nettie Phillimore's house," Lynda pointed out, munching on an unhealthful, trans-fat-laced potato crisp. "Maybe it's mostly a snooty social club. But I think you're being a little ADD here, Mac. Getting back to the coded message—"

"Yes, let us get back to that," Mac said. "Let us assume for the moment that it did come from Phillimore, meaning that the warning was genuine. To whom does it refer?"

"I vote for the Silver Fox," Lynda said without hesitation.

Mac raised an eyebrow.

"I mean Professor Ralston," my bride clarified. "She was full of praise for *The Valley of Fear* at Simpson's the night of the debate, and look at how many ways that book fits into this case."

"That's it?" I said. "That's all you've got?"

"Not by a long shot, darling. I've been thinking about this. Suppose that Carstairs really did kill himself, despite that business of calling his wife by her formal first name on his way out. Professor Ralston remembered the case because Carstairs worked for Phillimore—maybe she even knew him. Anyway, when she decided for some reason to kill Phillimore, she based his murder on his employee's suicide, right down to the suicide note by text.

"And here's the beauty part: She tried to convince us that the suicide of Carstairs was a murder, and the murder of Phillimore was a suicide!"

"That sounds like a mystery novel," I objected.

"Exactly!" Lynda said. "Isn't that just what you'd expect from the author of a book about mystery novels?"

She had me there, but I wasn't giving up.

"Why even bring up Carstairs?" I said. "We wouldn't have even known about him if it hadn't been for her."

"Because in that fairy tale she spun, Carstairs's murder provides the reason for Phillimore killing himself."

"And I presume that she killed Madigan because he had somehow ferreted out her guilt," Mac said. "That is the most common reason for the second or third murder in mystery stories."

Lynda nodded vigorously, sending her honey-colored curls flying. "Sure, it all fits." She smiled with satisfaction as she hoisted a pint of ale.

Mac stroked his facial forest. "Your theory is most intriguing and equally ingenious, Lynda. So why did she kill Phillimore?"

"Who knows? The motive could be financial or romantic—take your pick."

"Do we know that Ralston even knew Phillimore?" *Good question, Kate.*

"We can check it out, but I bet she did."

"Well enough to help him stage his disappearance?" I said. "We've been assuming that the killer did that. And why would Phillimore tell Madigan not to trust the Professor if it was Ralston? And why would she spell 'honor' in the American way if she was trying to make his death look like a suicide?"

"Maybe she did help him disappear, but then he realized she was up to something and warned Madigan. There had to be some kind of connection among Phillimore, Madigan, and the killer, whoever the killer was. Maybe the three of them were up to something together."

This was heading into Fantasyland, as far as I was concerned, and I tried to pull the conversation back to the real world.

"None of that explains why the veddy, veddy English professor would spell 'honor' in the American way."

Lynda opened her pretty mouth. Mac, Kate, and I looked at her expectantly. She paused. "Okay, I haven't figured that out yet," she said finally. "But maybe she's just a lousy speller. Do I have to do all the work for you guys?"

Excerpt from the Professor's Journal
June 13, 2012

*The elimination of Madigan, by far the riskiest of
several risky features of my plan, went off without a hitch.
Still, I have to admit that not all has gone according to
schedule. I had hoped that popinjay McCabe would be behind
bars by now. My effort to set him up has fallen woefully short.
With his admittedly formidable intellect free to focus on
finding the killer, I fear that I shall have to leave this
scepter'd isle sooner than I had anticipated. Perhaps I
miscalculated in involving him. Fortunately, everything is
ready. I can spring the escape hatch on a few hours' notice.*

Chapter Twenty-Seven
A Sea of Suspects

By the next morning, Lynda hadn't come up with anything better. And she didn't seem to appreciate me noting that.

"Well, who do you think the killer is?" she demanded, sitting crossed legged on our bed.

I wouldn't say we were arguing. Her yellow silk pajamas were too cute—not to mention form-fitting—for me to be arguing.

"Everybody's a suspect," I pointed out, "at least potentially. Let's list the possibilities and consider each one." Why hadn't we done this before? It made so much sense. I picked up the pad of paper thoughtfully provided by hotel management. Lynda would have typed on her iPad, but I prefer paper and pen, just as I prefer paper books to e-books. I started writing down names, saying them out loud as I wrote. Lynda helped, contributing names that I forgot.

The finished list looked like this:

Heather O'Toole
Nettie Phillimore
Roger Phillimore
Rod Chance
Aiden Kingsley
Trout
Sir Stephen Fresch
Margaret Carstairs

"Is that everybody?" I asked.

"Except for Ralston."

"Good. Let's just go down the names and see what we can come up with for each one. I'll be the prosecutor and you act as the defense attorney."

"Okay. This could be kind of fun." Lynda wiggled around to make herself comfortable. She has a nice wiggle.

This isn't exactly what I thought we'd be doing for fun in bed on our honeymoon, but okay.

"Heather O'Toole had a great motive to kill Phillimore if she thought she was going to inherit billions of pounds," I began.

Lynda shook her head. "She could divorce him with a lot less rigmarole and still walk away with a pile of money. Besides, why would she kill Carstairs?"

"They had a secret affair," I suggested.

"Puh-leeze, Jeff! When was the last time a successful movie actress killed somebody to cover up an affair?"

"She wasn't that successful four years ago."

"I still don't buy it. That's a Victorian motive for a post-modern world. I'm just talking reality. Tabloids like *The Daily Eye* live on that kind of sleaziness and it hasn't ruined anybody's career in decades. No, you can cross HO'T off your list."

Thinking that Roger Phillimore would doubtless be disappointed, I did so.

"On to Mrs. Phillimore number one," I said.

"There's another successful woman, and she already got her pound of flesh from Phillimore in the divorce."

"I think it was more like several million pounds of money," I quipped. "And that actually gives her a motive in the Carstairs killing. Suppose she knew all along about the Ponzi scheme and she killed Carstairs to silence him so that Phillimore's empire would be intact and he could settle millions of it on her at the divorce."

"But Carstairs died two years before the divorce. And then she waited until two years after the divorce and the start of a Scotland Yard investigation to kill Phillimore?" Lynda's voice was drenched with skepticism. "And how would Nettie know that Carstairs was about to blow the whistle? Whoever he'd planned to report it to, it sure wasn't Nettie Phillimore."

Who *had* Carstairs planned to inform? That was worth thinking about. Presumably he planned to go to the police, but if so he must have told the wrong person of his intention first. *Or maybe he went to the wrong cop.*

"And another thing," Lynda went on before I got very far with that line of thought. "Why would Nettie, of all people, help him disappear? We're assuming the killer was also the person who helped him do the Houdini, right?"

"Yeah, but maybe we shouldn't. That would rule out most people on the list—certainly Roger Phillimore, given the way he hated his old man."

"Or did he?" Lynda raised her eyebrows. "We shouldn't accept anything at face value. Maybe all that venom he directed at his father was just a show to throw Scotland Yard off the track. He could have been in cahoots with Phillimore in his fraudulent enterprises for all we know."

"Well, he is half-American," I said. "Maybe his mother taught him how to spell."

Lynda ignored my lame comment. "Suppose the younger Phillimore helped his father disappear because they somehow knew the police were closing in on him. James expected to leave the country and hide out somewhere, but Roger decided to kill him to make sure that his father could never turn against him."

"Okay, that all makes sense. Under this scenario, Roger also killed Carstairs earlier to keep him from blowing the whistle. But who's the Professor?"

"Professor Ralston! I don't suspect Roger Phillimore for a minute, Jeff; I'm just playing the game."

Suppressing a sigh, I put a question mark next to Roger's name.

"Next," I said, "we have Rod Chance, Heather's husband number one. He's a South African. How do they spell?"

"I don't know about that, but we'd have to assume an awful lot to keep him on the suspect list. Granted, he was one of Phillimore victims, so he'd have a nice revenge motive. But that doesn't get him anywhere near Carstairs or helping Phillimore to disappear."

"He could have been helping Heather. Maybe they were still a hot item. I've seen your parents in action." Lynda's parents have been divorced since she was a little girl, but whenever they get together they still . . . well, get together. When you're in a room with them you can practically feel the heat. You want to yell, "Rent a room!" But they can't be together for more than a week before the passion moans turn to Italian curses (Mom) and military oaths (Dad).

"Nobody is like my parents," Lynda said with a shudder. "Thank God and all the saints. But we've already ruled Heather out, so even if Rod Chance were still romantically involved with her he wouldn't be helping her kill Phillimore because she didn't do it. Besides, Faro reported in *The Eye* that Heather returned to the movie set in Barbados. I'm sure that if Chance went with her, Faro would have sniffed that out and reported it."

"Maybe that's why he didn't," I said. But I drew a line through *Rod Chance*. "How about Aiden Kingsley?"

"Oh, yes, our rising young Member of Parliament and brilliant but low-selling novelist. Nettie Phillimore has been boosting him strongly in *The Net* and we met him as he was coming to her place for cocktails and dinner."

"So were they getting together for business or monkey business?" I wondered aloud. "She's way older than he is, but that's no barrier. Did you read the story in *The Daily Mirror* this morning called 'The Caged Cougar'? It was about this forty-four-year-old office worker who sexually harassed her younger male colleagues at work."

"Whatever his connection with Nettie—and I personally think you should get your mind out of the gutter—there's the same objection as before: We've already ruled her out, so that should rule him out. He wasn't even a victim of Phillimore, according to Faro's list, so he has even less motive than Chance."

Scratch the M.P., reluctantly. My desire to see the little prig trade pinstripes for prison stripes was unworthy, but there it was.

"How about Trout, then?"

Lynda rolled her eyes. "The butler did it? You've got to be kidding."

"He may be a small fish in a sea of suspects, but if we were looking for the one person in this whole crew most likely to have helped Phillimore disappear, he'd win hands down. He was on Phillimore's payroll and he was in the house at the time."

"That's all true, but what about motive?"

I spread my hands, meaning "Come on!" "Getting the husband out of the way goes all the way back to David and Bathsheba. Trout works as butler, personal trainer, and part-time bodyguard to Heather O'Toole, which is quite a body to guard. Maybe he wasn't as uninterested in women as Heather thinks. Some people do go both ways, as the Scarecrow said in *The Wizard of Oz*."

Lynda stared at me. I knew my fly wasn't open because that wasn't where she was looking.

"What? What did I say?"

She shook her head. "Sometimes, Jeff Cody, I just marvel at the way your mind works. What about Carstairs?"

That stalled me, but only for a moment. "Maybe Trout killed him on orders from Phillimore to silence him. Phillimore planned the whole thing. Then Trout turned the tables on Phillimore four years later, killing him in exactly the same way because he didn't have the imagination to come up with his own plan." *Wait, that actually sounds pretty good.* "I'm not crossing his name off the list!"

"I don't think you should," Lynda said mildly. "You do realize, though, that the English-spelling business that works against Professor Ralston presents exactly the same problem for Trout as a suspect—and the last two names on our list as well."

"Sir Stephen is not a native speaker of English," I pointed out.

"No, but he's been in the UK a long time. He's more English than the English. I bet his British spelling is perfect."

"Well, he wasn't high on my list anyway. He has a good revenge motive, having lost a lot of money in Phillimore's scheme—never mind his reassurances to us about that—but I can't see him helping Phillimore disappear and I don't know why he'd kill poor Carstairs."

I drew a neat line through his name.

"So that leaves us with Mrs. Carstairs," Lynda said. "Take your best shot."

"Okay. Let's say she killed her husband—maybe there was a boyfriend in the wings."

"If so, he's still there. It's four years later and she hasn't remarried."

"Nevertheless, let's just say that's what happened and Phillimore figured it out. Maybe he liked Carstairs and never accepted the suicide theory so he kept poking into his death. Then, like a lamebrain in a mystery novel, he confronted the merry widow instead of going to the police.

She killed him the same way she did her husband because it worked the first time."

"And how about the disappearance of Mr. James Phillimore?"

"That was either a joke that Phillimore cooked up to amuse his friends or the first stage in skipping the country because he knew his house of cards was about to fall," I said. "Either way, it had nothing to do with Phillimore's murder."

"And Mrs. C somehow found out that he was holed up at the Langham, enabling her to go there and kill him?" The doubt in her husky voice was so thick you could cut it with a buzz saw. "And then she told us that her husband's suicide was a murder, which she apparently had also told the police?"

Lynda shook her curly head. "You're wasting your time on true crime, Jeff. You need to get back to fiction."

She lovingly removed the pen from my hand and crossed out the name of Margaret Carstairs.

"That just leaves us with Roger Phillimore and Trout," I observed, "and I put a question mark next to Roger."

Without comment, Lynda used the pen still in her hand to add "Professor Ralston" to the bottom of the list.

"We're back to where we started," I said. "Ralston doesn't work for me because I strongly suspect she knows how to spell and I don't buy your idea that Carstairs really did kill himself. You, on the other hand, seem to have a fixation about Professor Ralston. If I didn't know better, I'd think you were jealous."

"Jealous? Don't be ridiculous, darling." Lynda laughed—a bit hollowly, I thought.

Chapter Twenty-Eight
Bad Behaviour

When we met the McCabes for breakfast at the Pret a Manger closest to our hotel (a concession to me), Mac was engrossed in reading *The Daily Eye*. Faro's lead story carried the headline **TOP COP POPPED**.

"Typical tabloideze exaggeration," Lynda sniffed. "Madigan was only an assistant commissioner, one of four, by no means the top cop. I explained that in my story."

"Faro's piece below the headline is not exactly a model of journalistic restraint, either," Mac noted. He started reading aloud:

"Assistant Commissioner Andrew Madigan, a poor boy from Liverpool whose skill as a sleuth earned him a top position in the Metropolitan Police Service, was slain yesterday in his own home by a single shot to the heart from an American-made Colt .32 pistol. This reporter heard the gunfire and helped to find the still-warm body."

Mac continued for the next twenty-seven paragraphs. I still have the clipping of the story, so I could quote more, but you already know what happened at Madigan's house. In addition to the news of the day, the story contained a lot of background on the Phillimore case rehashed from Faro's previous epics.

"That's accurate enough," I said when Mac had finished, "but Lynda's story was better."

"Faro's sources—"

Whatever Mac was about to say about them was cut off by *The Ride of the Valkyries*. Mac answered his phone after a brief peak at the screen.

"Yes, Neville? Yes, I read as much in *The Daily Eye*. Well, I cannot say that I am surprised. Just now? And what do you deduce from that? I appreciate your confidence and I share your optimism. Indeed, all my instinct—and even Holmes talked about instinct—tells me that the solution is not far away. I promise you shall be the first to know."

Mac disconnected with a puzzled look on his face. "As I was about to say, Faro's sources at Scotland Yard clearly go beyond the late Assistant Commissioner. Inspector Heath himself just received confirmation that the murder weapon was a Colt .32—which, as you know, Faro already reported in this morning's newspaper."

Lynda expressed her frustration at the Anglo-American's scoop, using several impolite words. "We've got to figure this out so I can beat him on the big story."

Mac's eyes opened wide and he broke into a smile. "Yes, of course—the big story. That explains Carstairs, by thunder! Thank you, Lynda."

Whether he would have explained himself at that point is doubtful. But I'll never know for sure because he got derailed by Kate before Lynda or I could beg for more.

"Darned autocorrect," she muttered, completely oblivious to her husband's expostulating. Mac raised an eyebrow, which Kate couldn't see because she was working her smartphone with both thumbs. She expounded anyway. "I guess that's what I get for trying to be cute. I was writing to Mac's mother that I hope the kids are on their best behaviour—with i-o-u-r on the end, the British way—but my phone keeps correcting the spelling to i-o-r."

Mac thumped the table, shaking the water glasses. "I am an idiot! Why did I not think of that before? Phillimore's smartphone was British. It would autocorrect h-o-n-o-r to h-o-n-o-u-r. The person sending the message would have to retype the word to change the spelling back. That means the American spelling wasn't just a mistake. The killer wanted it to be that way—another false clue!"

This struck me as being brilliant, but possibly untrue. "Maybe he—or she—just automatically changed the spelling," I protested.

"That is highly unlikely. Most people do not notice autocorrects. Reflect on your own experience. How many times have you sent or received a text in which the phone had autocorrected one or more words to ludicrous effect?"

I looked at Lynda, almost blushing. A couple of weeks before our marriage, I had sent her a text in which the word "laptop" had been autocorrected to "lapdance." I hadn't noticed the change. Lynda had, to her concern.

"Good point," she told Mac dryly.

Kate pushed the "send" button on her smartphone and looked up. "Let me get this straight. The killer faked a suicide and then planted a clue in the suicide note to make sure that the police knew it *wasn't* a suicide? That makes no sense. Who would do that?"

"Someone with a very devious mind who wanted to indicate that the killer was an American," Mac said. "The unsuccessful attempt to frame me for Phillimore's murder was no afterthought. It was part of the plan from the beginning. This only confirms what I already knew, but it increases my confidence that I am on the right path. 'The thing takes shape, Watson. It becomes coherent.'"

"*The Hound of the Baskervilles*," Lynda said.

I stared.

"Well, I just read it two nights ago," she said defensively. "That was one of the books I picked up at the Sherlock Holmes Museum."

"But who would want to frame you, Sebastian?" Kate asked, sounding totally puzzled. She thinks he's totally loveable, of course, and has no clue as to his propensity for driving less tolerant souls crazy.

"It was probably some academic jealousy thing that Professor Ralston had going," Lynda said.

She gave a synopsis of our detective work that morning in talking through all of the suspects and crossing most of them off the list. I gave my best pitch for Trout, but Lynda still wasn't having it. She argued that Ralston was the strongest candidate of the three still in the running.

"And now that we know that the American spelling was a false clue, Professor Ralston—'the Professor,' get it?—is a better suspect than ever. She's English, trying to put the blame on an American. And take the business of committing the crime with the Colt .32. She would have known that Mac owned one from reading Jeff's books." Lynda turned to me. "I'm sure you remember that she made it quite clear that she was a fan of yours at dinner before the debate, the part where she was fawning and flirting." *Hey, not my fault!*

"And I'm sure you remember my previous objection," I countered. "Ralston argues that Phillimore's death really was suicide. The murderer wouldn't say that. Scotland Yard was only supposed to think it was suicide at first, but then realize it was murder and suspect Mac. That was the whole point of a suicide note with what we now know was a deliberate misspelling."

"Uh-huh." Lynda nodded as if I had proved her point. "That's just what the Professor wants you to think. Like Mac said, this killer has a very devious mind."

I groaned inwardly. This was like chess on steroids and I was about two moves behind. Lynda is smarter than I am, so maybe she was right. Mac seemed to agree. At least, I thought that's what he meant when he said, "I would like to speak with Professor Ralston again. I have a few questions for her. No, actually, I just have one question."

But he wouldn't say what it was.

Chapter Twenty-Nine
Hostage

Things moved quickly from there. Back at the hotel, Mac privately made what I later learned were three phone calls. Within fifteen minutes he was knocking at our door to tell Lynda and me that we were meeting some other "actors in this little drama" at the Brigadiers Club.

"Don't tell me you're handing Faro a piece of this story!" Lynda exclaimed.

"I assure you he is a most necessary participant."

"And why Fresch?"

"All will become clear very shortly, I promise."

Kate insisted on coming along because she wanted to be in on the end of the business, a desire that we would all soon regret.

A friendly, dark-haired young man in round glasses welcomed to the Brigadiers Club this time. He showed us into a small meeting room behind the morning room. Sir Stephen sat in a well stuffed chair. Inspector Heath and Welles Faro were settled in on opposite ends of a long leather couch. Curiously, Faro was still holding on to that fat book, *The Napoleon of Crime*, just as he had been the last time I'd seen him.

We all murmured the usual platitudes of greeting and shook hands before finding places to sit, Kate next to Faro and Mac on the other side next to Heath. Lynda and I claimed chairs.

My brother-in-law looked around, as if counting the crowd. "Well, we are all here, so let us begin."

"Wait a minute," Lynda protested. "Where's Professor Ralston?" She stressed the title slightly, a subtle nod to the mysterious "Professor" of the coded message.

"Althea will not be coming," Mac said. "She answered my question on the phone. All I wanted to know is whether the death of Peter Carstairs spontaneously emerged from her memory banks or someone reminded her of it. If the latter, you see, it could have been another plant, a false clue."

"And was it?" Sir Stephen asked.

I focused on the unlikely tycoon with his bald head, thick mustache, and faint Eastern European accent. And with a jolt it hit me: He must be the murderer. Why else would Mac have invited him instead of Ralston for this corny confrontation scene?

"No," Mac said. "Althea is convinced that she remembered the first murder on her own. And it *was* a murder, the first of three. Lynda gave me a singularly important clue when she referred to 'the big story.' I recalled then that Peter Carstairs used that very phrase, according to his wife."

He paused, as if he had just said something dramatic. We all looked at him blankly.

"Think about it," he continued. "When Carstairs talked to his wife about blowing the whistle on Phillimore's Ponzi scheme, he talked in terms of 'a big story.' Why did he do that? Because he planned to tell what he knew to a journalist, not to the police."

"But obviously he was killed before he could do that," Faro said.

Mac shook his head. "On the contrary. I believe that Peter Carstairs *did* tell his story to a journalist—who subsequently killed him. Have you ever noticed that reading habits tend to run in the family? Margaret Carstairs reads *The Daily Eye*. I would wager that her husband did as well."

"Good taste in that household then," Faro said with a forced chuckle.

It didn't work. I stole a glance at Heath. His body appeared tensed as if ready to spring. He hadn't yet said a word, and I had a feeling he wasn't going to. He was waiting for Mac to play this out.

Mac turned to Sir Stephen Fresch. "Sir Stephen, you approached me via e-mail with the happy thought that you and I engage in a debate here in London. Was that debate your idea?"

The entrepreneur looked slightly uncomfortable. "I never claimed it was, did I? No, it was Faro here who suggested it to me. To tell you the truth, he also gave me the winning argument. That was very clever of him, I thought."

"Oh, yes," Mac said, "Welles is a very clever killer."

"What!" Faro said. "Are you daft, man?"

Ignoring him, Mac continued to address Sir Stephen. "Did he also introduce you to Phillimore?"

Sir Stephen had to think about it. "Why, I'd almost forgotten, but yes, he did."

"I don't know the exact relationship, but somehow you were involved in Phillimore's Ponzi scheme, weren't you, Welles?" The coldness in Mac's voice sent a chill up my spine. "You killed Carstairs, Phillimore, and Madigan."

"That's impossible," I blurted out. "Lynda and I were with him when Madigan was shot. We heard the gunshot."

"Right you are," Faro affirmed with a smile. "I guess that's pretty much the perfect alibi. That should end this nonsense. "

"We heard a noise, anyway," Lynda said. "But Faro put the idea in our heads that it was a gunshot, didn't he?

And we never questioned it. I bet Madigan was already dead when you and I arrived, Jeff." *Now you tell me.*

Okay, that was unfair. Faro was the first person Lynda suspected. I'd pooh-poohed the idea, arguing that he wouldn't have written "honor" by mistake. And, of course, he didn't. We knew now that the killer did that on purpose. My logic as impeccable; it just led to the wrong answer.

"This is absurd!" Faro exclaimed with a great imitation of ruffled dignity. "Andy Madigan was a friend of mine. I was going to give him this book." He pointed to *The Napoleon of Crime*, sitting in front of him on a table. "It's a biography of Adam Worth, the real-life Moriarty." He opened the book—and pulled out a gun. He stood up and pointed it at Inspector Heath, the only other person in the room who was armed.

"Colt .32, I presume?" Lynda said. "You must have had it in that book the entire time we were in Madigan's house."

Faro smiled. "And Sebastian McCabe, Mr. Bloody Great Detective, didn't have the slightest idea, not to mention Scotland Yard."

Mac bowed slightly as if to acknowledge the gloat. "That part never occurred to me, I must admit."

Heath picked this moment to break his strategic silence. "You're a right bastard, Faro."

"Yes, and I would urge all of you to remember that." With sickening swiftness, he reached out his left hand and grabbed Kate by her right shoulder. "This gun, acquired along with its twin through the help of some Irish friends, has already fired one fatal shot. It still works. But as long as we all keep our cool and you don't attempt to stop me from leaving, the lovely Kate will be unharmed."

She pressed her mouth together, as if determined not to give Faro the satisfaction of showing fear. Mac wasn't that disciplined. For the first time in the two decades that I had known him, Sebastian McCabe seemed human.

The color drained out of his face. He looked like I felt—totally wrenched by the situation. "If you so much as bruise Kate—"

"You're in no position to threaten, you pompous bore. I was rather sure our meeting today would take this turn, but thank you for providing such an excellent hostage. Well, isn't somebody going to say, 'You'll never get away with it.'?"

"We'll leave the clichés to you," Lynda said. *Good one, Lyn!*

Faro's grip on the Colt tightened. For a moment, I was afraid she'd overreached. He seemed to be fighting to stay in control of his anger issues.

"I *will* get away with it, though. Don't you think I saw this day coming? I've had an exit plan for years, and today is the day to execute it. I've been ahead of you the entire time, all of you—the insufferable McCabe, the dullard Heath, and, of course, our relentless journalist Ms. Teal. I did kill Carstairs. Then I cut myself in on Phillimore's action and paid Madigan lavishly for protection. When the house of cards began to fall, I knew it was time to get rid of both of them. I decided to have a little fun with you while I was at it, McCabe. Pity that part didn't work out so well."

He began to walk backwards, pulling Kate with him.

"Unless you try something foolish, you'll get a call in a few minutes telling you where to find her. Goodbye, losers."

Chapter Thirty
The Wait

As Faro and Kate disappeared from view, Lynda said, "I never did like that asshole."

"What do we do now?" I said.

"The hardest thing possible," Mac replied, pulling one of his damned cigars out of his pocket. "We wait."

Kate is my bossy big sister, older by all of thirteen months, so I've known her all my life. When we were kids, it was Kate who told me to eat my vegetables, not my indulgent mother.

I waited as long as I could stand it, maybe another half a minute. "The hell we wait," I said, and took off running out the door and down the steps. Heath was right behind me. Despite my longer legs, the inspector kept up with me as I ran out the front door. Without saying a word, Heath peeled left and I went right.

The rain that had plagued our whole trip was just a drizzle. The concrete Pall Mall sidewalk was wet beneath my feet but fortunately not slippery. I suppose we had some vague, unspoken notion of trying to see in which direction they went, but no plan. It didn't matter. When I got to the corner I looked as far as I could in both directions and I didn't catch a glimpse of them.

Heath was shaking his head, coming from the other direction, when I got back to the Brigadiers Club.

By the time we rejoined the others, I had worked up a pretty good anger at my brother-in-law.

"If you knew that Faro was the killer, why did you bring Kate with you? She's the most innocent bystander in this whole mess. All she wanted was a nice vacation in London and now she's in the hands of a multiple killer."

Mac closed his eyes. "She wanted to be part of the denouement."

Lynda put a comforting arm around me.

"It never occurred to me that Faro would take such a drastic action," Mac added.

"That wasn't a good thing to not think of," I said acidly.

"You certainly underestimated the man," Heath piled on. He put down his cell phone, which he had been using to order up whatever Scotland Yard does when they want to follow a desperate man and not let him know that he's being followed. "Apparently you got the rest of it right, though."

Mac grunted. "That will be a bitter triumph if he harms Kate." He stuck the cigar in his mouth and smoked grimly, never mind the "No Smoking" law.

"How did you figure it out?" Sir Stephen asked, wiping sweat off of his bald head with a handkerchief.

"The real question is how I failed to figure it out sooner," Mac said. "And the answer goes back to Poe. Faro was hiding in plain site, just like the purloined letter in Poe's story. He had so many different connections in this case that we didn't even notice him. In addition to suggesting the debate and preparing you for it, Sir Stephen, Faro also arranged our lunch with Phillimore that was the prelude to his disappearance, after first putting the idea in our heads that we would like to meet him.

"After the disappearance and then the murder, he reported things that only the murderer or Scotland Yard would know. We assumed that he got all that from his source, presumably Madigan, but he did not. That is why he was able to confirm that the murder weapon was a Colt .32 even before Neville received the report."

"And before that," Lynda broke in, "he must have been the one who tipped Scotland Yard that you owned a gun identical to the murder weapon."

"The tip came in the form of an anonymous e-mail on a Yahoo account," Heath said.

Mac nodded. "I am not surprised. He sent you the message, Neville, and then reported it as if he had received the information from a Scotland Yard source."

I left the little room and hit the bar in the foyer. With no bartender in sight, I poured Lynda an Old Ben on the rocks—her second favorite brand of bourbon. I'd tell the club to put it on Faro's tab. It felt good to be up and doing something, anything, while we waited.

"He would have known about Mac's gun from reading my books," I said, handing Lynda the drink as I reentered the room. She smiled at me in silent gratitude. She looked like she could also use a cigarette, never mind that she'd quit more than a year ago.

"He also knew that Neville was a fan of my Damon Devlin mysteries—he had told me that," Mac said. "Therefore, he could be sure that his contrived parallels to my books *Nothing Up My Sleeve* and *Sleight of Hand* would suggest themselves to the inspector. He arranged for me not to have an alibi for Madigan's murder by getting us tickets to the theater. Kate was so grateful."

His voice cracked a little as he said that. I went back to the bar to fix myself a drink, bourbon and ginger ale. I don't care much for the taste, but I wasn't going to taste it anyway. There was a two-hundred-year-old clock behind the bar in the meeting room. The hands seemed to crawl as I waited for Mac's phone to ring.

"I do enjoy a good detective story," Heath said. "That's what bothered me from the beginning. It all seemed too much like a detective story."

"Faro shot himself in the foot by overplaying his hand," Mac said, mixing metaphors in a way he would never do in print. "His attempt to frame me not only failed miserably, it ultimately pointed right to him. His planted clue based on English versus American spelling, for example, almost had to have been dreamed up by someone who worked with words and was keenly aware of the language differences. Who else in this case matches that description?"

Lynda surprised me by saying, "Nettie Phillimore!"

That gave Mac pause. "By thunder, you are right! She is something of a wordsmith. However, she had no animus against me, no conceivable reason to wish that I should be suspected of her ex-husband's murder. The same goes for Althea, who lives by words as well."

"And what reason did Faro have?" Heath asked.

"I suspect that he held a juvenile grudge against me because I embarrassed him in a literary duel." Mac repeated the story he had told me some months ago about Faro and his theory that Holmes couldn't be Holmes without Moriarty. "Apparently he believed this quite passionately. He even gave his Sherlock Holmes group a name that referred to Moriarty, the Binomial Theorists." He studied his cigar. "And yet, at least two members of the group, Madigan and Kingsley, seemed to know and care little about Sherlock Holmes. That still bothers me."

"Who was the Professor?" I asked. "And how does the coded message fit in?"

"I do not—"

Mac's phone erupted. I was never so glad to hear *Ride of the Valkyries* in my life. The phone was sitting on the table in front of him. He hesitated, as if afraid of what news it might bring, then picked it up. "Yes? Thank God! I love you, too. Stay put. We shall be there in moments!"

He disconnected. "Kate is safe. Faro left her at Trafalgar Square and disappeared into the crowd."

Chapter Thirty-One
Ah, Love

"Look," Lynda said, "this is where we came in."

She pointed along the banks of the Thames at the Houses of Parliament and Big Ben, which we had first seen on our arrival in London.

It was just the two of us on a romantic cruise down the river. After what Mac and Kate had been through, they needed to spend some time alone. So did we.

If you're expecting me to tell you how Scotland Yard caught Faro at the border and stopped his escape, I'm sorry. He got away clean. Mac would have to wait a few days to have his few unanswered questions answered.

Meanwhile, I had my arm around my bride and she was cuddled up against me as we floated down the Thames. The river was high because of all the rain that month. Our guide pointed out the historic buildings along the banks, with informative and humorous commentary, as lights of the city shimmered on the river in the dusk.

During a lull in the guide's patter, I whispered in Lynda's ear:

"Ah, love, let us be true
To one another! for the world, which seems
To lie before us like a land of dreams,
So various, so beautiful, so new,
Hath really neither joy, nor love, nor light,
Nor certitude, nor peace, nor help for pain;
And we are here as on a darkling plain

Swept with confused alarms of struggle and flight,
Where ignorant armies clash by night."

Lynda pulled away a little to look at me. "What a load of crap. Where did you get that?"

"From Matthew Arnold, the English poet," I said. "It's the last stanza of his poem 'Dover Beach.' I learned it in high school or college, I forget which."

"Oh. I thought it sounded familiar. Well, I don't know who pissed in old Matthew's beer, but he had it all wrong—except for the first line."

"I think so, too. I've always loved the words but not the meaning, if that makes any sense. The world is not an easy place in which to live, but life is still pretty swell anyway."

"And that's a good thing because tomorrow we get on a plane and head back to the real world. This is the last official day of our honeymoon, *tesoro mio.*"

"That's right." I drew Lynda closer to me again. "Back we go to Oscar the grouch, the college, Ralph Pendergast, and my little apartment."

"And budget cutting, reporters who can't write, and publishers who don't understand what news is."

"I can't wait," we both said at once.

After a long flight to New York the next day and then on to Ohio, we arrived in town to find that Erin hadn't changed much. It never does. But somehow the seventeen steps to my carriage house apartment above Mac and Kate's garage looked higher than ever as we stood at the bottom with our luggage.

"Aren't you going to carry me over the threshold?"

As I have often noted, Lynda is a self-proclaimed "old-fashioned girl" and this would be the first time for us to enter the apartment as a married couple. We had spent our wedding night at the Winfield Hotel, where we'd had our reception.

"Sure, but let's put the luggage inside first." What I meant was, I didn't want to carry her up the steps. I work out, but so does she, and we all know that muscle weighs more than fat. So we dealt with the luggage and then I ceremoniously carried my bride inside our apartment.

After I put her down, we hugged and kissed and so forth for a bit. Well, it was more than a bit, actually. When we finally disengaged, Lynda looked around as if seeing the place for the very first time.

"It's good to be home," she said.

Chapter Thirty-Two
The Confession

Two days after we got back to Erin, Mac received the following e-mail from Welles Faro, sent from the address igotaway@bmail.com:

My Dear McCabe,

As you read this I am on my way out of Ireland, heading for the country where I will reside in considerable comfort under a long-prepared false identity. I intend to fully enjoy the fruits of my labours, the several million pounds I have deposited over the years in a numbered offshore bank account.

Having completely vanquished you in our little contest, except for the minor matter of you figuring out all too late that I was the player on the other side, I have magnanimously decided to answer a few questions you may still have. I've even attached an online journal of my thoughts, which you might find interesting. Despite your vaunted cleverness, I'm sure you don't know it all.

First of all, I'm the Professor. More on that later.

You may have learned by now that I left the United States fifteen years ago because the local authorities, not to mention my employer at the time, took a dim view of my hacking into voice-mails to get a story. The UK welcomed me with open arms, however. I suppose part of my success in Britain was the novelty factor. I was the outrageous transplanted Yank, and therefore I could get by with almost anything. I didn't give up my aggressive and sometimes-illegal journalistic techniques with the change of venue, but I found that even without them people were often willing to tell dear old Faro the most amazing things.

After a few years of this, I began to realize that some things I found out had more value than a leader in *The Daily Eye*. I wouldn't use the word blackmail, but neither did Charles Augustus Milverton.[3] I did a nice sideline in this for awhile. But when Carstairs came to me with the story of Phillimore's Ponzi scheme, expecting me to expose it in my column, I knew I'd hit the jackpot. All I had to do was kill Carstairs. Then I went to Phillimore and told him I would keep his secret, and even advance his enterprise, in exchange for a healthy share of the action. I told him that Carstairs was my source. The subject of his "suicide" never came up, but Phillimore either knew the truth of the matter or was even better at lying to himself than he was at lying to everyone else.

Within a year or so a kind of Stockholm Syndrome relationship developed between Phillimore and me. We became friends and partners. The sword I held over him was no longer mentioned. We discovered our mutual passion for Sherlock Holmes. I'd always admired the real Holmes of the stories, not the whitewashed image you have in your head. Holmes is no agent of the law. He is a law unto himself, which means that he is totally lawless. How many times does he commit burglary, set murderers free, and allow criminals to die before they can have their day in court?

But, of course, his shadow self, Moriarty, is my real hero. You would have understood that from my brilliant article if you hadn't been so focused on proving your own cleverness by shooting me down. The Binomial Theorists of London is not a Holmesian club at all, but what you might

---

[3] Editor's Note: The master blackmailer in "The Adventure of Charles Augustus Milverton," a Sherlock Holmes story.

call a Moriartian club, a kind of League of Criminous Gentlemen. Just as the head of the Baker Street Irregulars is called "Wiggins" after the young boy who led the original Baker Street Irregulars, my title as leader of the Binomial Theorists is "the Professor" in honor of our real hero.

Phillimore's trite warning to Madigan, "Don't trust the Professor," was the one genuine clue in this case—and it seemed to point to you! As you can imagine, I was surprised and delighted in equal measure. Call it a romantic impulse, but I had insisted that all members of the Binomial Theorists own *The Penguin Complete Sherlock Holmes* for just such a purpose as Porlock used *Whitaker's Almanack* in *The Valley of Fear*.

The Binomial Theorists afforded a convenient cover for me to meet with a number of collaborators without drawing any attention—especially Madigan, a bent copper with an expensive mistress. You may recall that his former boss, the commissioner, was criticized for meeting with executives and editors of *News of the World* for lunch or dinner several times during the Yard's investigation of the paper's phone hacking. But if Madigan and I happened to be together with Aiden Kingsley and other members of the Theorists for a few pints and a chat, what's the harm in that? Who would know that the others didn't really have an interest in Sherlock Holmes? Kingsley doesn't read anybody's books but his own, by the way, and he's on the take.

It was all going so smoothly . . . too smoothly. I was getting bored. I decided to take a bit of a risk. I stuck out my neck with my essay on Holmes and Moriarty—and you chopped it off. You must have been very proud of the way the other robots piled on in print. I decided to make you pay for that pleasure.

Just as I was trying to figure out how to do that, I got word from Madigan that the Yard was on to Phillimore. There was nothing he could do to derail the investigation, although he did manage to slow it down a bit. I gave you the impression that I'd first learned about it that day you saw me talking to Madigan at the Brigadiers Club, but he'd actually told me weeks ago, in a panic. He knew that if Phillimore went down, he would crack like an egg and we would all be in jeopardy. It was obvious that Phillimore had to go, just like Carstairs before him. I decided that he would go in a spectacular fashion that would engage your interest—and then I would frame you for the crime. Beautiful, isn't it?

First I lured you here with that debate—a debate in which I knew I could engineer your defeat and humiliation among your peers. Once you were here in the UK, I dragged you into the Phillimore case with the lure of the ACD notebook. I'm sending it to you under separate cover. I think you'll find it quite a good forgery.

The pastiche was designed to lead you to the priest hole and make you think it was your own clever idea. Maybe I went overboard with that reference to "the singular suicide," but I couldn't resist. I knew the clear reference to your dreadful *Nothing Up My Sleeve* would puff up your ego and keep you reading to the part I really wanted you to read. Then in Phillimore's house I sat on the window seat precisely to draw your attention to it. If you hadn't suggested looking there, I would have had to stumble onto it myself.

Of course, you were intended all along to figure out that Phillimore's death wasn't suicide. I knew that you would catch on to that "honor" right away. It pointed to murder, and by an American, but certainly not to me because I write in British English for a living. No, the American that it pointed to was you . . . especially after I thoughtfully informed the Yard about your ownership of a weapon similar to that used on the hapless Phillimore.

The irony was delicious: You couldn't help showing off by making the deductions that pointed straight to you. It was a kind of jujitsu, using your own self-satisfied cleverness against you. I had Madigan assign Heath to the Phillimore case because I knew he was a fool for that tripe you write and would immediately think of the double bluff in *Sleight of Hand* when you turned up clues that pointed to you. So what might have made you look like a less likely suspect did just the opposite.

And I'd provided you with a motive suitable for a Sherlock Holmes collector. The exchange of e-mails that I wrote between you and Phillimore should have clinched the case against you. Maybe Heath just didn't want to believe— another slight miscalculation on my part.

But I also didn't expect you to tumble onto Carstairs. I didn't think anybody would remember him, a nobody. I'll have to pay Ralston back for that some day.

Naturally, I tried to keep track of your actions without being too obvious. It helped that my irrepressible rival, Ms. Teal, accepted my Friend invitation on Facebook. When she posted a photo of what I recognized as Fresch's plane, I rushed out to Stansted to find out what you were up to. I was going to ask Fresch, but I encountered you first. Even better! By then I'd already decided how to get rid of Madigan. When he called me in a fresh panic and said you were asking about Carstairs, I knew that he had to go. Your reference that day to the delightful Kate gave me the idea of supplying you with tickets to the play so that you would have only the flimsiest of alibis for the time of his murder.

You'll remember how I at first dismissed the significance of Phillimore's message, until you deciphered it and it turned out to be one that could turn back on you, Professor McCabe. Then I shoved it right in Heath's face, but he wouldn't bite.

Even without knowing about Phillimore's warning to Madigan, I realized it wouldn't be easy to kill a veteran police officer who had reason to be wary. So I went well prepared, with the .32 hidden in the book and a trick up my sleeve. Not surprisingly, he greeted me at the door with his service revolver in his hand. We went to his den. Following my instructions, one of my Fleet Street Irregulars—a young man with a bottomless capacity for following orders without asking questions—set off a series of firecrackers behind the house. As I had anticipated, the noise startled Madigan. In the second that he jumped, I pulled out my gun and shot him, the noise indistinguishable from that of the firecrackers to any neighbors who might have heard.

Of course, the same young man set off one more firecracker about fifteen minutes later as I was standing outside the front door with your overeager sister-in-law and her neurotic husband—my alibis for Madigan's shooting.

When you asked me to meet with you that last day, I was almost certain that you were on to me. But I couldn't resist letting the scene play out to see how much of it you had deduced. You got very lucky, I must admit, but I was ready to move on anyway. All of my efforts since I decided to kill Phillimore were just aimed at buying time to get my escape plan ready to execute.

I think that's everything. This e-mail address was set up for this exclusive use and will no longer be monitored after I click *Send*. If you have any questions, you will have to ask them when we meet again.

And we will meet again, McCabe. Count on it. And when we do, I will destroy you. If you are wise, you will spend every day until then on the lookout for the return of the Professor, who I assure you will look or sound nothing at all like,

Yours truly,

Welles Faro

SHORT STORY BONUS!

The Adventure of the Vatican Cameos
Lynda Teal's Own Case

The body of Roberto Crocetti, 27, was found Monday in his apartment on the Via Monte del Gallo. The freelance photographer had been shot and his apartment ransacked, according to the police. There were indications Crocetti had been tortured before being killed, the police said. They suspect drugs were involved . . .
— *La Repubblica*, page 3, May 29, 2012

My husband, Thomas Jefferson Cody, is the most infuriating of men. Why do I put up with him?

Because he's adorable, of course! My friend Felicia once called him a combination of Woody Allen and Humphrey Bogart. I'd say he's more like Woody Allen *trying* to be Humphrey Bogart. But he's so cute about it.

Still, it was maddening that on the second day of our idyllic Italian honeymoon I was already forced to keep a secret from my new husband. Fortunately, what I didn't tell him did help me solve the thefts of the Vatican cameos. Oh, and the murder, too.

My road to deception began on that first night in Rome.

"What do you mean you want to read?" I asked Jeff.

"I always read before I go to bed." He held up a book, a Red Maddox private eye novel called *Bodies in Toyland*.

"We've been in bed for an hour, sweetheart. Haven't you noticed?" (If you're expecting any more details on that, you've come to the wrong place. Try one of those explicit Rosamund DeLacey romance novels that Jeff's wonderful administrative assistant is always reading.)

"I mean before I go to sleep," my redheaded and now red-faced darling clarified.

Well, I would have thought he'd be too worn out to read (*I* certainly felt relaxed), but apparently not. This presented me with something of a dilemma. I hadn't brought anything to read. A girl just doesn't think she's going to need a book on her honeymoon.

Totally fluent in Italian, thanks to summers spent in Italy with my *nonna* as a girl, I tried reading *La Repubblica* for a while to catch up on what had been happening in the world while I'd been otherwise occupied. The world was still a mess, and so was Rome—the usual mix of political crises, a young man murdered in his own apartment, an investigation of alleged police corruption, and even more depressing celebrity news (breakups of people I didn't know were together). Quickly tiring of all the bad news delivered in the world's most beautiful language, I closed my eyes and reflected with contentment on my first day back in the Eternal City.

We'd been married on Saturday and flown out of the Greater Cincinnati/Northern Kentucky International Airport on Sunday. After an enjoyable one-night layover in New York, we arrived in Rome at 11 A.M. Tuesday. It took more than an hour to get through customs. We finished just in time to find out that the cab drivers had all gone on a twenty-four-hour strike at noon.

"This must be why your grandparents left this country," Jeff muttered.

I rolled my eyes. "We'll take the metro to Termini station and walk from there to our bed and breakfast. It's not that far. The hike will make up for some of that lost time at the gym you were complaining about."

Jeff grunted.

We were staying just a couple of streets over from the Vatican Museums. At first Jeff hadn't liked the idea of a B&B, given what had happened the last time he stayed in one. But the price was too good to pass up and he is a cheapskate. My other suggestion was Madre Pie, but when Jeff found out it was a convent he wanted nothing to do with it.

On the way there we walked through St. Peter's Square.

"This is incredible!" Jeff said. "The pictures I've seen just don't do justice to the size."

"Uncle Guido always says there are two things the Church has plenty of: time and property."

Jeff chuckled. "Uncle Guido, eh? What is he, a Mafia don?"

Actually, he is Guido Cardinal Goldini, the patriarch of Venice. Three of his predecessors in the twentieth century were elected pope. Not all of my relatives are scandalous. But I didn't think Jeff was ready to learn about that particular branch of my family tree yet. I was trying to break him in slowly.

The hostess at our B&B, *Sogni d'Oro* (Dreams of Gold—quite a lofty name for a three-story building), was a vivacious, buxom, auburn-haired woman in her sixties named Sophia Belisamo. She was a real Roman; I could tell by the accent. My mother's family was from much farther north, hence the honey blond color of my curly hair.

We settled in, admired our ceramic tile floor and the view of St. Peter's dome, took a fifteen-minute power nap to stave off jet lag collapse, and then hit the bricks.

Why had I been away so long? The Eternal City is an eternal delight, and sharing it with Jeff doubled the pleasure. What is Rome? Rome is graffiti, gypsies, ancient buildings, even more ancient obelisks, cats, flowers, nuns in habits, priests in cassocks, dog dirt, motorbikes, crazy driving, tiny cars, double parking, political posters (fascist, communist, and anarchist), churches upon churches, pizzerias . . .

"And such beautiful, well-dressed women!"

That was Jeff talking.

"Down boy. You're taken."

I took his hand.

We dined that night at my favorite restaurant in Rome, Dino & Tony, at Via Leone IV 60, just a few blocks from our B&B. I suppose the hostaria-pizzeria has a menu, but I've never seen it. I always just sit down and stocky, effervescent Dino or one of his waiters (there is no Tony) starts bringing food—two plates of antipasti, two pizzas, two plates of pasta. And so it was on our first night in Rome. We passed on the main course to make room for dessert, which turned out to be tiramisu, caramel custard, coffee ice cream, and a plate of cannoli. Have I mentioned that we drank a carafe and a half of red wine with dinner, espresso with dessert, and limoncello to round out the meal?

"This was"—dramatic pause—"*fantastico!*" Jeff proclaimed with a contented look on his face and the last of the limoncello in his hand. That was Jeff Cody, linguist. And for a skinny guy, he sure can eat.

After two and a half hours of Roman food, we headed back to the B&B hand in hand across St. Peter's Square. I love the square at night, with the lights shining on the fountain and the obelisk. The obelisk, one of dozens in Rome, was already almost two thousand years old when the Emperor Caligula looted it from Egypt in 37 A.D.

I pointed up at a lighted window in the Apostolic Palace, my other favorite site. "That's the pope's apartment. I think the light means he's up there right now."

"I don't suppose he's watching—I don't know— *Fringe* or *Desperate Housewives?*"

"No, Jeff, he's probably reading a Sherlock Holmes story."

On the pleasant memory of that zinger, I fell asleep with Jeff's light still on.

The bed was fine, but the continental breakfast was a bit of a downer. There was nothing wrong with the self-served food provided by Signora Belisamo—croissants, Nutella, yogurt, fruit, coffee, and the like—but the other guest who joined us at the table put a damper on the morning. She was in her early twenties, blond, about my height. If she'd been wearing makeup it would have been smeared. I could tell that she'd been crying.

As soon as she gave us a mouse-like "good morning," it was obvious that she was an American. That made it easy for me to start a conversation with, "Where are you from?"

By drips and drabs I got it out of this rather plain young woman that her name was Amber Kidwell, that she had just earned her master's degree from an art school in Illinois, and that she had a job lined up with a museum in Savannah, Georgia, starting in mid-June.

"I like your cameo," I said, pointing to a necklace that hung a bit incongruously over her ancient Grateful Dead T-shirt.

She started bawling.

I looked at my husband. "Jeff, do you want to get the maps and stuff ready for our day?"

He had a mouthful of Nutella-smothered croissant. "I'm still—" I glared. "Oh, sure. Right. I'll be right back."

"No hurry." This girl needed help.

As soon as Jeff had gone, taking an apple with him, I said to Amber, "Tell me about it, dear."

"My boyfriend—or maybe he's not my boyfriend—disappeared without a word. Oh, I've been such a fool!"

His name was Roberto. Presumably he had a last name, too, but Amber didn't know what it was or where he lived. They'd met in the Museum of the City of Rome and things had moved quickly. He'd proclaimed his undying love for her, practically moved into her room at *Sogni d'Oro*, and given her the cameo necklace as a gift. It was a locket, and she'd planned to put his photo inside, but he never gave it to her. "And I haven't seen him since he left here on Sunday. I should have known! I was nothing more than a fling for him. But he was so charming."

Yes, Italian men are that. Not well known for their fidelity, however.

"Oh, you poor dear!" I moved my chair closer and put my arm around her. Here I was all of thirty, married four days, and I was acting like her mother. "Men are such a trial."

I thought of my own somewhat tortuous path to marriage. Jeff is the communications director for St. Benignus College, a small Catholic institution in our little town of Erin, Ohio. I'd been a reporter at *The Erin Observer & News-Ledger* when we'd met. I kept taking him out to lunch, allegedly to talk about stories. I guess I was being too subtle. It took him forever to get around to asking me out. For weeks all I got out of him was calls pitching story ideas. I was on the verge of taking matters into my own hands when he finally cracked and saved me the trouble. After a mere five years of dating, not dating, and sort of dating, we had ended all that nonsense with a beautiful wedding.

"You didn't have a fight?" I asked Amber.

She shook her head, bouncing her blond hair. "No, everything was fine when he kissed me goodbye on Sunday morning." I suspected he wasn't on his way to church at the time.

"Did he seem different—moody, depressed, secretive, anything like that?"

"No more than usual. He was always a little mysterious. That was part of his charm. He kept telling me he was a poor photographer but he was about to come into some big money." She gave a rueful chuckle. "I didn't believe it even then. Maybe he didn't believe it himself—or maybe he did. I just don't know."

Something about this missing photographer was nagging at me, a feeling that I should be remembering something.

"If I knew where he lived, I'd march over there and give him a piece of my mind," Amber said.

My bet would be that he'd have a perfectly logical explanation and seduce her all over again.

"Well, since you don't know where he lives, you might try the 'plenty-of-other-fish-in-the-sea' approach. Rome is full of men. Just be more careful next time. Have you ever thought of maybe wearing a little makeup, just a hint of color here and there?"

We were deep into practical advice along those lines when Jeff returned wearing his backpack and St. Benignus College baseball cap. The only thing missing was a sign saying "TOURIST!" But he looked really cute.

"Enjoy your day," Amber said, standing up. "And thanks, Lynda. I feel a lot better now."

This was our Vatican day. We toured the totally awesome St. Peter's Basilica, attended the papal audience at noon, and visited the Sistine Chapel, which no words can do justice. The way out of the chapel led us through a gift shop run by the Daughters of St. Paul. I wandered away from Jeff there and bought a cool Vatican shot glass with an image of St. Peter's to go in my shot glass collection.

A few blocks outside the walls of the Vatican, we found ourselves in front of the only kind of store where Jeff Cody is likely to actually spend money—a bookstore.

"Hey, I can pick up a book for Mac," Jeff said. "Let's go in."

That was perfect for me.

Sebastian McCabe is Jeff's best friend and also married to Jeff's sister, Kate. He's an exuberant, larger-than-life character, amusing and aggravating, different from Jeff in almost every way. Although his day job is professor of English literature and head of the popular culture program at St. Benignus, McCabe is better known in several languages as the author of the popular Damon Devlin mystery novels. His books are old-fashioned mysteries in the manner of Agatha Christie or Ellery Queen. Jeff, on the other hand, labored for years without success to write in his favorite mystery subgenre—the hardboiled detective. I think he's given up on that, though, now that his books about his adventures with McCabe have been published.

McCabe's ultimate hero is Sherlock Holmes. So naturally Jeff feels compelled to sniff at the sleuth of Baker Street. Thus my little deception—when Jeff wasn't looking, I bought a paperback copy of *Racconti di Sherlock Holmes*, a collection with twenty of the short stories, for my night reading. If he knew what I was up to, he might feel that I was taking sides against him. I certainly didn't want to hurt his feelings, but we were meeting McCabe and Kate in London next week and I wanted to be prepared for the whole Sherlock Holmes thing. Strangely, I'd never gotten around to reading the original stories, although I'd seen some movies.

Guiltily, I paid for the book and looked for Jeff. He had a digest-sized comic book in his hand. "What's that?" I asked.

"*Dylan Dog*. It's Mac's favorite Italian comic book. He calls it a graphic novel, but it's a comic book."

We had dinner that night at Da Roberto, a crowded, noisy, and wonderful restaurant at Via Borgo Pio 62. Our waiter, Claudio, had lived in Cleveland for eleven years.

"I have a little a surprise for you," Jeff said over the gnocchi. He handed me a small box.

Well, what woman doesn't like surprises that come in small boxes? And when I opened it, I was overwhelmed.

It was a cameo necklace. "You admired Amber's, so I thought maybe you'd like one," Jeff said. "I bought it at the Vatican gift shop while you were getting your shot glass."

"Oh, Jeff!" I started crying. First of all, it was a wonderfully romantic gift. I would always remember that he bought it for me on our honeymoon. Plus, I was moved that he shelled out for it. Jeff Cody has never been known to throw his money away. He still has the first dime he ever earned—and it's probably grown to ten or twenty dollars by now through prudent investment and compound returns.

"You can put my picture in it," he said.

When we got back to *Sogni d'Oro*, the place was in an uproar. I suspected something was wrong when I saw the police car outside, a blue and white Alfa Romeo 159 with the words *Polizia di Stato* on the side.

Inside, our fellow guest, Amber, was dissolved in tears once again and our buxom hostess, Signora Belisamo, was talking with a police officer in rapid Italian. He was about a foot shorter than me and kind of cute. They were going too fast for me to catch most of it, but I did get the word *rovistato*—ransacked.

The officer, whose name was d'Annunzio, turned to Amber and spoke in heavily accented English with the air of one going over something one more time. "And you are sure that nothing was taken?"

She nodded. "Absolutely. I told you, everything I brought with me fit in a duffle bag. After six years in art school, it's about all I own."

Amber was still wearing the cameo necklace. In other circumstances I would have felt awkward; no two girls want to be dressed the same.

It turned out, as the women explained after the *agente* of the *Polizia di Stato* had gone, that someone had broken into Amber's room during the day and ransacked it, as if looking for something. She was shocked to find the mess when she returned to her room from a day of visiting museums and trying to mend her broken heart.

"Why me?" Amber asked with a sniffle. She hadn't taken my advice about the makeup. "I don't have anything worth stealing. I don't even have a boyfriend!"

That was a non-sequitur, but she was upset. I put my arm around her and tried to give some comfort. By the time Jeff and I had children, this mothering thing would be old hat for me.

"Does that happen a lot in Italy?" Jeff asked as we closed the door of our room a few minutes later. "I'd like to know whether I should hide my valuables."

"You don't have any," I said distractedly. I had a feeling I should be worrying about something other than being burglarized, but I couldn't put my finger on it.

Later, while Jeff was reading his private eye novel, I dove into *Racconti di Sherlock Holmes* over on my side of the bed. If Jeff somehow got the idea that I was reading an Italian romance novel, well, I didn't set him straight. Within a few minutes of starting "*Uno scandolo in Bohemia*," I was utterly lost in Sherlock Holmes and his world. This was bad, very bad. How could I explain to my husband that I was captivated by this rather cold Englishman who he'd made up his mind to treat with indifference at best?

Halfway through the second story, *"L'uomo dal labbro spaccato,"* I realized what had been bothering me. The word *rovistato* from Signora Belisamo's conversation with the policeman shows up fairly often with the meaning of "overturned." But how did I know that it also has the less common meaning of "ransacked"? Because I'd looked it up last night in the Italian-English dictionary on my smartphone, that's how. It was part of a story I'd read in *La Repubblica* about a young man who'd been killed and his apartment ransacked. And he was a photographer—like Amber's boyfriend! I couldn't remember his name, though, and I'd thrown the newspaper away. I decided I'd better not tell Amber. She was already distraught enough, and I might be wrong. I tried to concentrate on Sherlock Holmes.

We rose early the next morning and didn't see Amber at breakfast. I was wearing my new cameo necklace over a white blouse with a scoop neck. An Austrian couple named Dieter and Mitzi, perhaps in their mid-fifties and far from newlyweds, chatted with us in excellent English. They'd already been to most of the iconic Roman sites on our day's itinerary—the Coliseum and Forum, the Pantheon, Trevi Fountain, etc.

When we stepped out of the B&B after breakfast, right away I noticed something that struck me as strange. There was a man squatting on the sidewalk across the street. He was short, swarthy of skin, and dressed in rags. And yet he looked familiar. Had he been there yesterday? I didn't think so. "Jeff, I think that gypsy's watching the building," I whispered. "And he's talking into a cell phone."

"Everybody's talking into a cell phone," my darling responded in an exaggerated whisper of his own. "This is Rome. And gypsies are everywhere. You're just paranoid because of the robbery. Don't let it get to you!"

His first two statements were true; his third was not. That gypsy was definitely looking at *Sogni d'Oro*. And what if he wasn't a gypsy? The second story I'd read last night, "The Man with the Twisted Lip" in English, was about a man who disguised himself and went out begging every day while his wife thought he was going into the City to do whatever it is that business people do in London. Maybe the gypsy look was just such a disguise. But I couldn't very well tell Jeff that. He would ask me where I'd gotten such a crazy notion, and then I'd have to tell him about the Sherlock Holmes book I was keeping out of his sight. Oh, what a tangled web we weave . . .

We started our day's activities with a bus trip that eventually got us to the Pantheon, the largest surviving temple of ancient Rome. Once converted to a Christian church, today it is the resting place of the Italian kings Umberto I and Vittorio Emanuele II. Nearby we visited *Santa Maria Sopra Minerva*, a church built on top of a pagan temple. From there it was on to the *Colosseo* and, after lunch, the *Foro Romano*.

"I wish I'd studied harder in that Roman literature class in college," Jeff said. "One trip to Rome isn't enough, is it?"

I shook my head. "No way, sir. That's why we're going to the *Fontana di Trevi* next."

You know the tradition: If you throw a coin in Trevi Fountain, you will return to Rome. I was taking a picture of Jeff standing in front of the fountain, tossing the coin behind him, when I felt a tug at my neck. For a brief moment I thought I was being strangled. Then the chain on my necklace broke. I lowered the camera and turned my head just fast enough to see a man in a blue shirt disappearing into the crowd.

"Hey! Stop!" Jeff yelled, and tore off after the thief.

I knew better.

I sat down and waited for Jeff to return.

He was panting when he came back. "The bastard knew the side streets. I'm sorry, Lyn."

I put my hand on my ample chest where the locket had been. My husband followed the hand with interest. "This is awful, Jeff. I feel violated. No wonder Amber was so upset."

To think of Amber was to connect the two robberies in my mind . . . and maybe the murder of Amber's boyfriend . . . and the man watching our bed and breakfast. Where *had* I seen him before?

I kept these musings to myself. Jeff already thought I was paranoid.

"At least the necklace can be replaced," Jeff said bravely. But I could see him mentally adding the unexpected cost to the day's expenses.

We agreed that there was no point in calling the police. Signora Belisamo had a different idea, however.

"*Polizia! Polizia!*" she insisted.

She made the call.

The representative of the *Polizia di Stato* who showed up was of surprisingly high rank for a petty street crime. *Ispettore Carlo Petrocelli*, his business card said. He was dressed in a tailored suit, middle-aged, with a high forehead. He oozed charm and expensive cologne. This guy was no Columbo. I strongly suspected that he visited a mistress during the mid-day break when most businesses in Italy shut down. Many Italian men did, if they could afford it.

"And did this cameo have a special value?" he asked.

"It sure did." I looked at Jeff, who was eyeing Petrocelli as if the inspector had cut in on his date at the prom. Marriage had not completely cured his sometimes-annoying, sometimes-endearing tendency to be jealous. "It was a gift from my husband." I pointed at said spouse.

Petrocelli's eyes widened almost comically. *"Marito?"* he repeated. Husband?

"Sì, marito!" What was so surprising about that? Judging by the statistics, I guess getting married is a bit old-fashioned, especially in Europe. But I'm an old-fashioned girl. I explained that I was a newlywed, *una sposina*. He looked even more puzzled. Something was getting lost in translation here, even though we were speaking the same language. Maybe I wasn't getting the Roman dialect as well as I thought.

"This stolen necklace is a locket, *sì?"* Petrocelli asked.

"Sì."

For about two seconds I wondered how he knew. But after a moment's thought, I realized that there must be approximately forty-two million similar cameos around the necks of visitors to the Vatican.

"Well, I hope there was nothing of sentimental value inside."

"No, nothing," I said. "It was empty. I didn't have a chance to put my husband's picture in it."

The questions went on for a few more minutes. Did it have any distinguishing marks? Where did it come from? Could I describe the robber? Were there any friends with us who witnessed the robbery? As we talked I wandered over to the window and looked out. The gypsy was still there. Should I tell the inspector? What, and get the same skepticism that I'd gotten from Jeff? I just wished I knew why the man across the street looked so familiar.

Petrocelli wrote down all my answers with great precision as if there were actually a snowball's chance in hell that I would ever see my cameo again. It was great theater. But by the time the inspector left, I was worn out. We went to our room.

"I'm going to take a rejuvenating shower," Jeff announced.

"Okay. I'm going to read a bit."

It turned out that Jeff thought his shower would be even more rejuvenating if I helped him. After a playful but brief discussion, he headed dejectedly for the shower and I picked up *Racconti di Sherlock Holmes*. I lay down on the bed and read *"L'avventura dei sei Napoleoni"* —"The Adventure of the Six Napoleons." When I'd finished the story, I closed the book and sat up. I was getting an idea.

The back story of the adventure, the part we don't know until the end, is that a thief has hidden an especially valuable pearl inside a statue of Napoleon. Later, he steals and smashes a bunch of similar statues to try to find the one with the pearl inside. Sherlock Holmes being on the case definitely spoils his day.

And I started to think . . .

My cameo, like the statues of Napoleon, wasn't that special by itself, except to me. There would be no reason for somebody to risk ripping it off my neck in public to get it— unless there was something in it! I knew there wasn't, of course, but maybe the thief at Trevi Fountain didn't know that. Suppose this all had something to do with Amber and with Roberto's murder, if that's what it was. I couldn't fit it all together, I was moving too fast for that, but somehow I intuited that it did fit together. I needed to talk to Amber. She still had her cameo. Maybe there was something in it that she didn't know about. After all, it had been given to her by Roberto, who was now out of the picture.

There was a pounding on the door—the bathroom door.

"Hey, Lyn, the door is stuck. I can't get out. Can you help me?"

It was a sliding door. I looked down and saw that a screw had come out of one of the bottom glides. The loosened glide had twisted, wedging the door in place.

"Um. I'll try. Just wait a minute. I have to do something. Practice putting down the toilet seat lid for a while." Jeff always forgot that, which was quite annoying in the middle of the night.

I left the room, trotted downstairs, and knocked on Amber's door.

"Who's there?"

"Lynda."

When she opened the door, I could see that she'd been lying down on the bed for a late-afternoon nap. She was wearing another retro tie-dyed T-shirt, The Doors this time, and no necklace. Her blond hair was mussed.

"Sorry to bother you," I said quickly, "but I wonder if I could look in your locket."

"But there's nothing in it."

"Well, maybe not, but let's see."

She picked the necklace off of a dresser and handed it out to me as if she disdained it. "You can have it. I never want to see it again. Men are such pigs."

I opened the locket. There was a memory card for a camera inside. "What's that doing in there?" Amber asked.

"I think Roberto must have hidden it there. Do you have a camera?"

"Sure."

We put the memory card in the camera. Several of the pictures were vibrant street scenes, a few showed Amber and a handsome young man who I presumed to be her lost boyfriend, and two were the reason the card was hidden. They showed a man I recognized in close conversation with another man who must have been someone important.

"I know why your room was searched and why my necklace was stolen," I told Amber. "I'll explain very soon." I also knew for sure now what had happened to Roberto, and it was going to be hard to break that to her gently.

I put on Amber's necklace, with her permission, and went back to our room.

Jeff was still stuck. I pushed on the door and rotated the glide back into position so the door would slide open.

You'd think Jeff would be grateful to be liberated. "Where the hell have you been?" he fumed.

"If I answered that now, it would be the beginning of a long explanation that we don't have time for. Put on some clothes and meet me downstairs. I'm calling Petrocelli."

I smothered his objections with a deep kiss—amazing how that always works with him—and ran out of the room, leaving him there in his undershorts.

On the ground floor I looked out the window. The gypsy was still there. I called the phone number on the business card Petrocelli had given me.

"*Ispettore*, I think I have something that you're going to want to see."

"Where are you, *signora?*"

He promised that he would only be a few minutes, and he was as good as his word. In fact, he arrived just after Jeff. I had no time to prepare my poor husband for what was about to happen.

We met Petrocelli outside.

"Your cameo!" he exclaimed. "You recovered it. You are better than the police. How did this happen?"

"Come with me," I said.

Without giving him a chance to answer, I marched across the street and right up to the gypsy.

I handed him the cameo necklace. "I think you'll want to see what's inside there. And I also think you'll want to arrest Inspector Petrocelli."

Petrocelli's hand moved quickly toward the Beretta concealed by his tailored suit coat. For a second I thought I was going to have to give him a practical demonstration of Tae Kwon Do. But the gypsy was quicker. His gun was out in a flash and aimed at the inspector. "I believe we are in your debt, *Signora*," he told me.

"So, Petrocelli was a crooked cop and the gypsy was an honest cop," Jeff said over dinner at Dino & Tony. We were drinking wine and waiting for the first wave of antipasti.

I nodded. "You know I'm better at faces than at names. I would have recognized him right away as the *agente* that investigated the burglary in Amber's room if it hadn't been for the dark-skin makeup.

"He was all part of an investigation of police corruption. I read about that in *La Repubblica* on our first night in Rome, but I didn't pay attention to it, just like I didn't pay any attention to the story about poor Roberto's murder."

"So they killed him because of this photo he took of Petrocelli meeting with a well-known Mafia boss?"

"Right. A lot of this is speculation, but apparently Roberto was taking some atmospheric shots for a magazine piece at some out-of-the-way pizzeria a few weeks ago. He recognized the Mafia guy, Barzini, when he took the picture. Later on, he saw a picture of Petrocelli in the paper and he realized the importance of a picture of a police inspector breaking bread with a Mafia don. He tried to blackmail Petrocelli."

Jeff winced. "I could have told him that wasn't a good idea."

"No, it was a terrible idea. Petrocelli's minions followed him to our B&B, then to his apartment. Under torture, he finally admitted that he'd given the memory card with the incriminating photo to his new American girlfriend, hidden for safekeeping in a cameo locket. That's what Petrocelli's thugs were looking for when they tore apart her apartment. When they didn't find it, they decided she must be wearing it. They'd never seen Amber, so when they saw a tallish blonde come out of our B&B wearing a cameo necklace, they just assumed I was her."

"But didn't they think it was a little strange that Roberto's girlfriend was with another man?"

"Well, Petrocelli certainly was thrown for a loop when he found out I was married and you were with me at *Sogni d'Oro*. But maybe his minions didn't know anything about Roberto; that would be the smart way to play it."

"And Petrocelli just happened to be the investigating officer when your necklace was ripped off your neck?" Nobody does sarcasm like Jeff Cody.

"He arranged it that way, silly. That would have been a clue if I were looking for clues—to have an inspector investigate a minor street crime didn't really make sense."

"Why was the younger cop—d'Annunzio, wasn't it? —watching the house?"

"If I understand this correctly, the higher-ups already suspected Petrocelli. He was under surveillance when he met with Roberto. When Roberto was killed not long after, they were sure that Petrocelli was behind it but had no proof. They told the media that the murder involved drugs, as duly reported by *La Repubblica*, to lull him into a false sense of security. When Amber's room was ransacked, they assumed—"

"Wait a minute," Jeff interrupted. "How did the police know she was Roberto's girlfriend?"

Dino and a waiter set down two trays of antipasti with a flourish. After they left, I said, "They'd followed Roberto for a while because they had no idea who he was and they thought he might be somebody important. So they'd seen him go into *Sogni d'Oro* with her. Anyway, when Amber's room was searched the *Polizia di Stato* figured the robbers were Petrocelli's thugs who had been looking for something that they didn't find. So they assigned d'Annunzio to watch the place in disguise in case they came back."

"And you saw through the disguise," Jeff said.

"I was pretty sure it was a disguise, but it took me long enough to figure out who was beneath the makeup."

"But you did it! And you figured out that cameo thing, too." He chuckled. "Who needs Sebastian McCabe with a super-sleuth like you around?"

I thought of my hidden copy of *Racconti di Sherlock Holmes* that had provided me with the inspiration. My little deception.

"Um, actually, I had some help. I've been meaning to tell you about that. More wine, *tesoro mio?*"

A FEW WORDS OF THANKS

My wife, Ann, and I visited London with friends just a few months after the McCabes and the Codys. It was much as Jeff described, although we could never find the King Charles Hotel. Jeff and I owe a special note of thanks to (in chronological order):

Roger Johnson, who introduced us to Speedy's over a delightful lunch and who read this book in manuscript form, doing far more than I asked;

Steve Emecz, my publisher, who took our whole crew to dinner at the Sherlock Holmes Pub;

Robin Rowles, who gave us his Red-Headed League Tour of London;

Paul Austin, who showed us the Reform Club, and Tim Symonds, who made that possible; habitués of the Reform Club will note that it has similarities to the Brigadiers Club in this book, but also differences.

In addition, I wish to thank as usual the others who read, proofread, and commented on this work before publication: Ann Andriacco, Kieran McMullen, Jeff Suess, and Steve Winter.

This book was improved immeasurably by their efforts. The mistakes that have escaped their eagle eyes were probably added later by Jeff Cody or by yours truly.

About the Author

Dan Andriacco has been reading mysteries since he discovered Sherlock Holmes at the age of nine, and writing them almost as long. The first three books in his popular Sebastian McCabe – Jeff Cody series are *No Police Like Holmes, Holmes Sweet Holmes,* and *The* 1895 *Murder.* He is also the co-author, with Kieran McMullen, of *The Amateur Executioner.*

A member of The Tankerville Club, a scion society of The Baker Street Irregulars, since 1981, he is also the author of *Baker Street Beat: An Eclectic Collection of Sherlockian Scribblings.* Follow his blog at www.danandriacco.com, his tweets at @*DanAndriacco*, and his Facebook Fan Page at www.facebook.com/DanAndriaccoMysteries.

Dr. Dan and his wife, Ann, have three grown children and five grandchildren. They live in Cincinnati, Ohio, USA, about forty miles downriver from Erin.

Sebastian McCabe, Jeff Cody, and Lynda Teal will return in
Art in the Blood

THE
AMATEUR
EXECUTIONER

DAN ANDRIACCO
KIERAN MCMULLEN

Fascinating collaboration with Kieran McMullen, the
leading historical Holmes novel writer.

Also from MX Publishing

Visit www.mxpublishing.com for dozens of other Sherlock Holmes novels, novellas, short story collections, Conan Doyle biographies, Holmes travel books and more.

MX Publishing is the award-winning world's largest independent Sherlock Holmes Book publishers with over 50 new authors and 100 new Sherlock Holmes stories in print.

Benedict Cumberbatch, In Transition
The definitive performance biography.

CPSIA information can be obtained at www.ICGtesting.com
Printed in the USA
LVOW01s0455120713

342559LV00011B/301/P